T0077928

Murder at Desert Lakes HOA

CHUCK WALKO

authorHOUSE

AuthorHouse™
1663 Liberty Drive
Bloomington, IN 47403
www.authorhouse.com
Phone: 833-262-8899

This is a work of fiction. All of the characters, names, incidents, organizations, and dialogue in this novel are either the products of the author's imagination or are used fictitiously.

Published by AuthorHouse 06/06/2022

ISBN: 978-1-6655-6101-3 (sc)
ISBN: 978-1-6655-6102-0 (e)

Print information available on the last page.

This book is printed on acid-free paper.

Contents

Chapter 1

✦✦✦✦✦

Melissa pulled the top of her overcoat closer and leaned her body into Jamie. Her shivering may have been because of the cold drizzle or the horror she had just experienced. February rains in the Arizona desert can be chilling to the bone and create a dense, eerie fog in the night.

Jamie and Mellissa Roberts watched in silence as the two bodies were placed in the ambulances. Four police cars still had their lights flashing. Steve Donavan of the Pinal County Sheriff's office was still interviewing witnesses off to the side. Bob Graves of the Casa Grande Police, who had questioned Jamie, went back to his car and was busy on the phone. He had asked the couple if they wanted to keep warm in his vehicle because he didn't want them to leave the scene in case he had any more questions while he called into his office, but they both wanted to be with the people who still lingered outside the community center. They wanted to assist those who had experienced the trauma of the evening. They wanted to know if their son-in-law, Donavan Rice, was alive or dead.

The couple headed to a small group that surrounded Santiago Montoya, the Buildings and Grounds Manager, and his wife Juanita to offer them some succor and at the same time get support for themselves.

All the conversation was about Donavan Rice. Would he be taken alive to the hospital or be placed in a bag as the other two victims of the shootings were? As soon as the police and paramedics arrived, they immediately cleared the auditorium and began working on Don, who was lying face-up on the floor in a pool of blood. Melissa was screaming and crying profusely and demanded that she stay with Don, but one of the men helped Jamie to forcefully drag her from the scene as more equipment was rushed in for his survival.

Bob Graves got out of the car and spoke rather solemnly to the Roberts.

"I've called Casa Grande Regional to send for another ambulance. It should be here within thirty minutes. The emergency room there will be ready to begin whatever surgery or care Mr. Rice needs. The medics inside have been in touch with the hospital. Your son-in-law has lost a lot of blood and still has a bullet stuck in his right arm which must be removed in emergency surgery. He is still unconscious, but the medics feel that he can make it to the Medical Center."

Melissa, who was still sobbing, grabbed her husband's hand. "Thank God!" Wiping away tears, she looked at Jamie sadly and whispered, "Should we call Robbie?"

"No, not yet. Let's wait until we know for sure he'll survive at the hospital and what his condition is before we try to contact Robbie. Besides, I don't even know where Robbie might be. Last I spoke to him, he said he was flying a charter to Jamaica for the Mardi Gras there."

"Okay. He told me also about going to Jamaica for a week. I don't know when he'll be back in Arizona. Oh, my God! Just when both boys are doing so well, this has to happen." In between sobs she uttered, "Robbie will be devasted if Don dies. We all will!" She paused to catch her breath. "Can you imagine that crazy son-of-a-bitch killing Randy and … God forbid… our Don!"

Jamie's wife of more than thirty-five years broke down crying again. He had never seen Melissa so distraught. He held her tightly and fought back tears himself. He too felt her anguish and disgust at the meaningless loss that had occurred at their homeowners' association meeting. For Don to be shot down at the prime of his successful law career was beyond comprehension. He knew that Melissa was right: Their son Robbie would have a complete breakdown if he lost his partner and the love of his life for over fifteen years.

"I better call Cee Jay," he said, grabbing for his flip phone. "He's probably concerned about all the sirens and flashing lights."

Cee Jay picked up the phone on the first ring. His voice was tense.

"Jamie, what's going on down at the Club House?"

"I don't know if you heard it yet, Cee Jay, but Maxwell shot Randy and Don….."

Cee Jay yelled before Jamie could continue. "Don!" There was a long silence as he tried to gain composure. "How is he?"

"We don't know yet if Don will survive. The medics are transporting him to Regional. After Maxwell shot Randy, he aimed at Don, but Don managed to fire a shot at him that killed him. Melissa and I will be following the ambulance to the hospital."

"Give me three minutes to put on some clothes. I was just getting into bed when I heard all the sirens. Do you want me to meet you at the hospital?"

"No. We'll swing by and pick you up. You can ride with Mellissa and me. Just be out front."

"Jamie, does Robbie know yet?"

"No. He's in Jamaica with a charter. Melissa and I want to know if Don will make it before we try telling Robbie. Cee Jay, I see that they're bringing the stretcher out now. Got to go!

Pick you up in three."

Melissa and Jamie rushed over to get as close to the ambulance as possible. He was glad that Don's face was attached to an oxygen mask as opposed to covered with a sheet. That meant that he was still alive. The ambulance siren and flashing lights lit up the night fog as soon as the doors were secured, and without hesitation, he grabbed her hand to lead her to their car. She was shivering.

"He's going to make it, honey" was all he could say as he started the engine. Mellissa burst out in tears again.

"How?" she stammered through sobs. "Why? Jamie, why did this have to happen?"

Jamie leaned over and kissed her forehead. "I don't know, baby. Whatever happens to Don, it's all part of God's plan. We have to trust in God and be strong in that belief for Don, Robbie, Cee Jay, and ourselves. We can pray for Don, but must accept without any bitterness what the outcome of this night will be." He gazed into his wife's loving eyes. At that moment his love for her seemed more than he could bear. They had been together for all but sixteen years of their lives, had two children, and two grandchildren. They had experienced great joy and many sorrows, but their love for one another grew greater every day. Jamie knew that he was truly blessed.

"How did Cee Jay take it?" Mellissa asked.

"I think he was in a state of shock, but he's going with us to the hospital."

As the car started, Mellissa wiped the tears from her face and eyes. "Poor, Cee Jay. He loved Don as a father."

"Yes, Don was really the son that Cee Jay never had. That bond started in high school but grew stronger over the years."

Cee Jay lived on the other side of the lake and on the main road leading out of the Desert Lakes community. He was already at the end of his driveway when Jamie drove in. Without speaking, he got into the back of the car. Melissa extended her hand to him which he grabbed. The three of them were lost in their own thoughts and sorrow to speak for most of the twenty-minute drive to the hospital.

When they got off the Interstate 10 at Florence Boulevard, Cee Jay broke the silence. "I was thinking of the day that we drove Don and Robbie down to Rutgers. You know that's when he started calling me Dad. I loved him like a son, and now…" Cee Jay began crying profusely. "Why? Oh, God, why?"

Jamie parked near the emergency entrance. Turning off the ignition, he quickly got out of the vehicle. He opened the back door for Cee Jay and grabbed his arm to help him out. Melissa got out on her own and walked around the car to meet them.

"I'm afraid to go in," Cee Jay cried. "I don't want to hear it."

Jamie put his arms around Cee Jay's shoulders and Melissa put her arm around his waist. The automatic doors separated as they approached. The waiting room was empty except for two men who were huddling in a far corner. The group went directly to the receptionist.

"May I help you?" she asked with a warm smile.

"We are the family of a man who was just brought in from Desert Lakes," Jamie said.

"Yes, Mr. Donovan Rice is in surgery now."

"What is his condition?" Melissa asked.

"I really don't know yet," the nurse replied. "Dr. Fernandez will meet with you after he comes from the OR. If you would like, you may be seated and wait."

"Do we have any idea how long we will be here?" Cee Jay inquired.

The receptionist smiled. "I really have no idea, but I'll inform Dr.

Fernandez that you will be here. There are vending machines over there if you would like coffee and snacks. The two gentlemen over there are also waiting for the report on Mr. Rice's condition."

"Thank you," Jamie said to the nurse. He led Cee Jay and Melissa over to the seating area.

As soon as they were seated, the two men approached. They did not recognize either of the men. The taller and younger man extended his hand to Jamie. "I assume you are Mr. Roberts."

Jamie stood and shook his hand. "Yes. And you are?"

"My name is Bill Gonzales. I'm a reporter for the **Casa Grande Gazette.**"

"And I'm Guy Neville of the **Tucson Star.**" He and Jamie also shook hands.

"Tucson, huh? Don't you have enough crime down there to fill your paper?" Jamie sarcastically asked.

"Well, this story is a bit unusual. It isn't often that we're called on to report a murder story at a homeowners' association meeting. Especially, when it happens in a nice, quiet, model community of people such as those at Desert Lakes."

Guy Neville quickly interrupted. "And especially when the crime involves a prospective candidate for the United States House of Representatives." He paused. "Mr. Roberts, we know how upsetting this has been for you, but we would appreciate your answering a few questions. If it's okay."

"I know it's your job, so I'll be willing to tell you what I can. First off though," Jamie said, "as for Don Rice running for the House, he has not yet announced his candidacy. He has just established an exploratory committee to test the water."

"Yes, we know that, but the Democratic Party is prepared to give him the nod."

Bill Gonzales asked the next question. "Will this incident tonight ruin Donavon Rice's position? We understand that he did fire the gun that killed one of your residents?"

The question was upsetting to Jamie. "God damn it! The man is being operated on as we speak. I don't even know if he's going to live, and you guys want to know how this may affect his potential run for political office. Jesus Christ! Don shot and killed the man who shot him first. And that son-of-a-bitch shot and killed the president of our homeowners' association. Don was acting in self-defense. If Don pulls through this, he will have to decide himself if he can run for the office." Jamie turned to the others. "This is my wife Mellissa and this man is a long-time friend of the family, Dr. Cee Jay Seton. Dr. Seton was the first president of the Desert Lakes HOA. He has been Don Rice's mentor since high school." Gonzales spoke next. "Seton? Aren't you a professor at CAC?"

Cee Jay stood and shook his hand. "Yes, but I am only an adjunct instructor at Central Arizona College." He also shook hands with Guy Neville from the Tucson paper. "I have to agree with Mr. Roberts. We hope and pray tonight- or rather this morning- that Donavon will survive and if he does, he will have to decide about considering his future in politics. If he does, however, I can tell you that Arizona will be getting an outstanding man in Don Rice."

There was a lull in the conversation before Melissa spoke. "We have known Don since he was in high school." She paused momentarily. "Do you know that he is our son-in-law?"

"Yes, we are very well aware of his relationship to you," Guy Neville said. Seeming as if to change the subject, he said, "Is it true that he was responsible for building Desert Lakes?"

"Well, he did create the concept, chose the land, and acted as my attorney in all matters concerning Desert Lakes; but it was my company, Roberts Development, that supplied the financing and actually did the construction and sales. But I will admit that the community's success was because of the hard work and genius of Don Rice. We had worked together on a smaller community in northern New Jersey before taking on the Arizona project at Desert Lakes."

"Can you tell us more about the incident last night? Apparently, there was a shouting match that got out of hand. One of the residents argued with the Board of Directors about an issue over solar panels. Mr. Rice, as the Board's attorney, gave an explanation which the Board agreed with. Robert Maxwell, a resident who was killed by your son-inlaw, didn't agree and shot and killed the HOA president, a..." Neville checked his notebook. "a Mr. Randal Scott, who also died at the scene."

"That pretty much sums up last night," Jamie said; "but the argument over the use of solar panels was started by Mr. Maxwell two months ago. Maxwell was demanding that John and Alysa Jumison, who had solar panels installed on their roof, remove them. After Don Rice explained that Arizona law protected the Jumisons' use of solar energy at a public Board meeting last month, Maxwell went door-to-door throughout the community.

"He got a substantial number of homeowners to sign his petition against solar panels. His position was that the value of all the homes in Desert Lakes was negatively impacted by the- what he called- 'unsightly appearance' of the panels. He even got a real estate broker to support this opinion. Maxwell and a friend also concocted a crazy idea that fire insurance rates were going to increase because of panels causing fires and that the panels created waves that caused cancer. The Board rejected the petition, and Randy Scott told Maxwell that he was wrongfully inciting the community to cause an unlawful insurrection. That's when Maxwell took out his gun and the shots were rapidly exchanged." Jamie paused momentarily.

"I believe Robert Maxwell was a trouble-maker and problem for us from day one,"

Jamie continued. "He even was on the Board for a short time until, at Mr. Rice's suggestion, the Board voted to remove him. They did, but that's when every meeting was monopolized by Maxwell's bitching about everything. The solar panel issue was just the latest one that ignited the fuse."

The reporter for the Casa Grande paper shook his head. "It's a bit weird that he didn't complain about ham radio and television antenna and heating and air conditioning units on the roofs."

"In planning Desert Lakes, we deliberately put everything underground," Jamie explained. "There are no overhead electric or telephone wires in Desert Lakes. We also had Direct TV install cable to every home to eliminate antennas. We built our homes with heat pumps deliberately to avoid the old, loud, big ground air conditioning units. The heat pumps were deliberately set back from the front view of all the homes. Unfortunately, we didn't know about and, therefore, did not consider newer technologies such as solar energy." He chuckled. "We are, though,

I believe, the only private community that offers a runway for small airplanes, helicopters, and hot air balloons."

"Now, gentlemen, if you will excuse me. I want some privacy with my wife and friend as we await the surgeon's report on our son-in-law."

Almost in unison, both reporters presented Jamie with their business cards, thanked him and asked if they could call his office, if necessary, for further information about the incident, Mr. Rice's condition, and his running for the House of Representatives. Their departing words were, "We'll keep Mr. Rice in our prayers for his complete and quick recovery. And thank you also Mrs. Roberts. Dr. Seton."

We watched the newsmen leave the hospital. "Well, that went well. I think." Melissa said.

"Let's see what the afternoon editions will say," Cee Jay replied.

Jamie sat down again. Melissa sat in the middle. He noticed that she and Cee Jay were holding hands, so he grabbed her other hand and held it firmly. They were silent, lost in private thoughts and emotions.

A door near the reception desk opened and a young, good-looking man dressed in hospital garb and a surgical cap walked over to them. "I am Doctor Fernandez. I understand that you have been waiting for word on Mr. Rice's condition."

"Yes, I am Jamie Roberts, this is my wife Melissa, and Cee Jay is our family friend of many years. Don Rice is my son-in-law."

"First, let say how sorry I am for all that you must have been through last night. It must have been quite a blood bath at Desert Lakes last night. Two men were pronounced dead at the meeting and Mr. Rice suffered a serious gunshot wound to his upper arm. He lost a lot of blood. That and the trauma accompanying such a wound would have killed a man a few years older and less in physical shape. The bullet was still in his arm when he was brought in so I had to surgically remove it and repair the blood vessels in his elbow. That was the tricky part and I'm hoping that after recovering he will be able to use his arm again. What I am most worried about and what we will have to keep a good watch on for the next several days is that while he was on the operating table, he had a pulmonary embolism. This condition is not unusual when a patient has lost as much blood as Mr. Rice did and had low blood pressure in a main artery. He will be in an induced coma state for at least two days. We'll keep him in intensive care for the next two days. I listed his chances as stable but cautious."

Melissa spoke first. "When will we be able to see him?"

"Frankly, Mrs. Roberts, you would not want to see him. He's wired up to so many tubes and respirators you wouldn't recognize him anyway. He, of course, is in a comatose state so he would not know you were present. I suggest that you go home, have a good sleep, and let the nurses and doctors in the IC unit keep a watch.

"If you want, the nurse at the desk here can give each of you a mild sedative to help you sleep. Give her your names, relationship with the patient, and telephone contact numbers. You can also call here in the late afternoon for a medical update on his condition. You will not be able to visit with him until he is moved into a regular hospital room. Only immediate family members are permitted in intensive care. I'm afraid that regulation excludes in-laws and good friends." The doctor's smile was friendly but condescending.

"By the way, is your daughter aware of this? As his wife, she could be with him in IC for short periods of time."

"Oh, we do have a daughter, but she is married to someone else and lives in Pennsylvania. When I said Don Rice was our son-in-law, he is; but he is legally married to our son. Robbie, my son, is a pilot and is currently in Jamaica and no, he does not yet know about his husband. We wanted your prognosis before trying to contact him."

Doctor Fernandez smiled more genuinely. "My bad. I just assumed.

But I do understand." He emphasized the word 'do.' "You should let Robbie know as soon as possible. I'll alert the staff so they don't make any mistakes as I just did. Please accept my apology."

"No problem. Happens all the time," Jamie said. "Robbie and Don have been together for fifteen years."

"That's great! I hope all goes well and I'll be seeing both of them during the recovery.

You folks go home now and get some rest. Don't forget to talk to the reception nurse here, for a sedative."

They did get the sedatives and gave telephone contact numbers before leaving the hospital. Jamie noted the clock behind the receptionist's desk. It was four a.m.

9

Chapter 2

✦✦✦✦✦

Jamie Roberts was standing in the kitchen trying to get the coffee machine to complete its cycle. He was still in bedroom slippers and a bathrobe. He had a vague recollection of Melissa getting out of bed, but must have immediately rolled over and fallen asleep again. He had no idea what time it was.

"That sedative really helped you, I see." Melissa was fully dressed and sitting on a barstool across the room. She was working on a sudoku puzzle. "Did you hear me getting out of bed?"

"Yeah, sort of; but I fell asleep again. How long have you been up?"

"Only about an hour. It's two in the afternoon." She pretended to get back to her puzzle. "Would you like me to make breakfast for you? I already had coffee and a few rolls."

"Not right now, honey. Maybe later, after I've had a cup or two of coffee. Has anyone called yet?"

"No. We should give the hospital a call. Then try to get Robbie down in Jamaica."

"I'd like Cee Jay to be here when I talk to Robbie. Also, I think I'll want Barbie to be in on the call. Maybe she knows a way to reach Robbie."

Their daughter Barbara, whom everyone called Barbie, lived in Frenchtown, New Jersey, with her husband, Greg Otenburg, and their two children, Gregory "Junior" and "Missy" who was named after Melissa.

Jamie knew that the relationship between his two children was a very close one. Even though they lived far apart now, they were in frequent contact. Perhaps it was because Robbie and Don loved doting over the children and Don and Cee Jay held a close bond with Greg, who also was a professor of English at the college in Doylestown, Pennsylvania. Greg was an avid golfer who got Cee Jay, Don, and Robbie interested in the sport.

The coffee was overly bold. After a few mouthfuls, he had enough. "I'm going to take a shower. Hopefully, it will wake me up better than this awful brew. Honey, why don't you make a new pot for the two of us, and I'll have a roll or two before I call the hospital and Barbie."

The land developer felt the cool water flowing over his body and stimulating his senses. The events of last night flashed before him, but suddenly a question loomed large over the event. *Yes, Donovan did shoot Maxell; but how could he? Don didn't own a gun. If he had, I would have heard about it. Either he or Robbie would have said something. As far as I knew, Don seemed against gun ownership, and yet the police did say they checked and Don did have a registered gun in his name. He would ask Cee Jay if Don ever told him that he had a gun*

Turning the shower off, Jamie decided that he would call Cee Jay first.

He noticed that Melissa had set the morning room table for two. She was pouring the coffee when he entered the room. "Do you feel better?" she inquired. "You certainly look more like the man I married."

"Thanks. Melissa, did you know that Don had a permit to carry a gun?"

"No. Last night I was surprised to learn that he not only had a gun, but knew how to use it."

"Strange. The same dawned on me while I was in the shower. Don't you think we would have known?"

"Definitely! You can't keep a thing like that a secret in this family." Jamie immediately started dialing Cee Jay.

"Morning, Cee Jay. I hope I didn't wake you."

"No. I've been awake for some time. I was just going through my files looking for something that I archived that Don wrote while he was still in law school."

"Cee Jay, did you know before last night that Don had a gun?"

"Interesting that you should ask that question. No, I didn't; and that's why I'm looking for Don's old paper. He wrote an argument against gun ownership and the Second Amendment for a class. I helped him with some of it, and we discussed it at length. He presented a brilliant argument. That's why I made a photocopy of it. I'll bring it over later."

"Good. Come here as soon as you find it. I really would like you to be here when I talk to Robbie."

"Sure thing, Jamie. I'll be there in about half an hour. I hope Melissa has a big pot of her self-ground coffee waiting. Have you called the hospital yet?"

"No. Not yet, but will as soon as I hang up with you. Then I will call Barbie and Greg to let them know. Perhaps they will help get me through to Robbie in Jamaica. Bye."

His hand was shaking as he dialed the hospital. *Please God, please. Let him be alive and well.*

The woman who answered the call introduced herself as 'Nurse Kira in Intensive Care.' She sounded more officious than friendly and reassuring. "Yes, Mr. Roberts, Donovan Rice is still in the IT unit. He has been placed in an induced coma. His condition is listed as 'Stable but Critical.' We do not expect that there will be any changes in his status today. Do you have any other questions, Mr. Roberts?"

"Do we know yet, if Mr. Rice will be able to use his right arm?"

"I really am not in a position to answer that question. Perhaps, when he is conscious, the doctors will be better able to determine that."

Jamie thanked Nurse Kira and hung up. Melissa put her arms around him, and he kissed her gently on the cheek. "I guess in this case, no news is good news."

"I should call Barbie and Greg now. It must be a little after five in Pennsylvania now. They both should be home."

Barbie quickly answered the phone. "Dad, what a pleasant surprise!" He could hear his two grandchildren in the background. It seemed that one of them was crying and the one was laughing.

"I hope that I'm not calling during your dinner or at a bad time."

"No. No. Any time you call, is a good time, dad. It's just a typical day here at Otenburg-ville." You now, kids yelling, screaming, running around. I'm going crazy, but loving it. Dad, were Robbie and I this much trouble when we were kids? So, how's mom?"

"She fine. She is right here beside me and we are on speakerphone." "Hello, dear."

"Mom, what's going on? I can tell by the sound of your voices that something is wrong."

"Barbie, I'm calling to tell you that Donovan is in the hospital. He was shot last night at the HOA meeting."

"Oh, my God. What happened? How is he?"

"A man who lives here… his name is Robert Maxwell… shot and killed Randy, the HOA president, and then shot Don; but Don was able to shoot and kill him. Don was operated on at Casa Grande Regional last night and is in intensive care."

"Oh, my God! This is so horrible. Were you there?"

"Yes, your mother and I were there to witness it all. Cee Jay wasn't, but he did go with us to the emergency room. We waited until we were able to talk with the surgeon. Don was hit in the elbow area of his right arm but also suffered a pulmonary embolism. He is in intensive care and his condition has been listed as stable but cautious."

"How has Robbie taken all of this?"

"Robbie doesn't know yet. As you probably know, he flew a group to Jamaica for the Mardi Gras."

"I spoke to Robbie just yesterday. You know my brother. As usual, he said he was having a blast. He'll have a breakdown when he hears about Don."

"Barbie, you said that you spoke to him yesterday. Do you know how to get in touch with him down there?"

"Yes. At Don's demand, Robbie finally got a cell phone. If you hold on a minute, I'll get the number for you. Hold on." She put the phone down and Jamie heard more sounds of the children playing. He also detected Greg's voice in the background. For a moment he felt envious of Greg because he remembered the joy that Barbie and Robbie brought to his life when they were as little as his grandchildren.

Barbie gave him Robbie's cell number and carefully instructed him on making an international call. "Dad, you said that Don shot and killed Maxwell. I didn't know that Don owned a gun let alone how to use it to kill a man in the crisis situation you described."

"I know, baby, that has all of us puzzled. Apparently, he didn't even tell Robbie."

"A few months ago, Don told Gregory and I that he was considering running for a position in Congress; and that if he won, the first thing he would do is initiate legislation limiting gun ownership. And now this….

It's crazy."

"I know. Cee Jay is baffled by it also. He's coming here in a few minutes with a paper that Don wrote on the Second Amendment while he was still in law school." Jamie paused for a moment to gather his thoughts. "Barbie, when Cee Jay gets here, I will put Robbie on speakerphone so your mother and Cee Jay will be in on the call. May I call you back so that you and Greg can also be in on the call to Robbie? I'd like this to be a family gathering if you will. Robbie should know that the entire family is here to help him deal with this."

"Great idea, dad! I'll let Greg know and we will try to keep Junior and Missy quiet."

"Thanks, Barbie, I appreciate that. I'll call you again in about half an hour when we're ready to call Robbie. Bye for now."

Jamie turned to Melissa. She had started crying again. "You know this will be the hardest phone call I hope I ever have to make. How does a father tell his son that his spouse is in the hospital and may or may not live? God, give me strength."

"He will, Jamie. You had the strength and bravery years ago to tell Robbie about Cee Jay, and now God will help us through this." Just at that moment, the doorbell rang. "Speak of the devil! That must be Cee Jay."

Opening the door, he noticed that Cee Jay looked haggard and confused. His eyes were bloodshot as if he were crying for a long time. He had not shaved. Jamie also noticed that he was carrying a file folder; it probably contained Don's paper. As Jamie drew him in, he kissed him on the forehead and then longingly on the lips. Once in the living room, Melissa kissed Cee Jay.

"I'm sorry, but I must look a mess. I haven't slept a wink."

"Well, you got some terrible news last night, so you deserve to look as bad as you do." Melissa chuckled and smiled. "I just had an image of how handsome, tall, and happy you were when you walked Donavon down the aisle and gave him away to our Robbie."

"You mean that silly event that was more of a class reunion because I had taught most of the guests, including the two best men? The event where Jamie had a silly grin during the wedding and at the reception insisted that he would only dance with gay men who were friends of the grooms?"

"Yes, that event." Melissa turned and gave her husband a dirty look.

"You didn't have to remind me of Jamie's antics, but I know that Robbie will be glad that you are here with us now."

"Cee Jay, I called Barbie before, and she and Greg will be on speakerphone also. If you are ready, I'll call her back now."

"Fine, let's do this."

It was Greg who answered the call. "Hello, dad. Barbara told me what happened to Donavon. We are shocked and saddened to learn this. Hello, also Mother Roberts and Cee Jay. If you can hear me okay, I guess it's time to give Robbie the word." Brief greetings were exchanged before he hung up momentarily to call Robbie. As soon as his phone started ringing, he placed the phone back on speaker so everyone could hear.

"Dad!" Robbie's voice was filled with his usual exhilaration. Robbie's enthusiasm for life was so pronounced, he could keep talking and asking questions before you say hello. "What's happening in Arizona? Dad, you and mom should come down here for some R 'n R. The people here are beautiful, the beaches are beautiful, and Jamaican rum is oh, oh, so good. And Mardi Gras here is a blast. Better than New Orleans! I'm having the time of my life! You got my new cell number, so you must have been talking to Barbie. Not even Don has it yet, even though he was pestering the hell out of me to get one, and when I do, he doesn't pick up."

"Robbie, Barbie is at home in Pensy, but I have her and Greg on speakerphone. Your mother and Cee Jay are also in on this call."

"Sounds like the whole gang is there." The tone of Robbie's voice changed immediately.

"But you didn't mention one member of the family who should be there: Don. Is something wrong, dad?"

"Yes, son. There is. And it concerns Don."

"What about Don? Did something happen to Don?"

"Don is in the hospital in Casa Grande, Robbie."

"Hospital! Why? What's wrong with him?"

"He was operated on last night and into this morning for a gunshot wound he received at the Desert Lakes HOA meeting."

"Oh, God! No! That can't happen! Not to my Don! Mom, tell me Don's okay."

"Oh, honey, we are so sorry. We are praying that he will survive, but we just don't know yet."

"Cee Jay, are you there?"

"Yes, Robbie, I can hear you."

"Level with me, Cee Jay. How badly was he hit?

Cee Jay spoke calmly, but forcibly with as little emotion as possible. "He was hit in the right arm, near the elbow. The bullet was removed at the hospital, but he lost a lot of blood."

"What about his arm?" Robbie fired. "Will he be able to use it?"

There was a pause as they looked at one another trying to decide who should answer this question. Both Melissa and Cee Jay deferred it to Jamie. "As of an hour ago, we don't know. The surgeon said it's too early to make that decision. Robbie, Don is in intensive care and is in an induced coma. Right now, the major concern is that while in surgery Don suffered a pulmonary embolism. The embolism seems to be the most serious aspect of Don's condition at present."

"For god's sake, tell me what his chances are to stay alive!" Robbie shouted into the phone.

It was the two-year-old, Missy who was the youngest member of the family, who was heard next. "Uncle Don-Don be okay. We pray he be good," she said.

This broke the tension a bit, and the three people in the room smiled.

Robbie spoke to his niece in a loving manner that was not condescending. "Thank you, Missy, for your prayers. Promise me that you will continue to pray along with your mommy, daddy, and brother for Uncle Don-Don."

It was Junior who, when he was just learning to talk, had difficulty saying Donavon, so he called him "Don-Don." Soon everyone in the family was referring to him as "Uncle Don-Don," and Donavon delighted in the appellation.

"Dad, was Roger Pucket at the meeting last night?"

"No. Why do you ask?"

"If he wasn't at the meeting, he must be on assignment. I thought that he could fly down to Jamaica and take my place here to fly the charter group back to Tucson. I'll try to get coverage so I can get home ASAP. Dad, it may be easier for me to hop on a flight going to Phoenix rather than Tucson, where my car is. If I get into Sky Harbor, could you pick me up there?"

"Of course, son. Just call when you know." He added, "Day or night and what time."

"Thanks, dad. I want to be at Don's side when he comes out of the coma. We will all have to be close to our telephones. Thank you, family, for your best wishes and prayers for my man. Bye for now."

Barbie was the first to speak after Robbie was off the phone. "That was better than I expected. I thought Robbie would have a screaming and crying fit. He actually seemed a lot more composed than I would have given him credit for."

"I attribute that to his pilot training," Cee Jay said. "A pilot must quickly assess the situation and immediately take whatever necessary steps he can without letting emotions get in the way. That quality also is what made Robbie a champion basketball player in high school. With emotions running high and a lot of screaming and yelling around him, he was able to keep calm and do what was necessary. He'll have time later for his own emotions after everything is processed. I understand that about Robbie."

"I agree with Cee Jay," Greg said. "Robbie handles things very well. Certainly, better than I can. Knowing Robbie, he'll manage somehow to be in Arizona by this time tomorrow."

"Thanks, Greg, Barbie, and you, too, Junior and Missy. Pray for Uncle Don-Don. And also pray for your Uncle Robbie because he will need to be extra brave and courageous while Uncle Don-Don gets better. Love you. Stay in touch. I'll keep you posted. Bye for now."

After a minute or two, Melissa spoke. "So, guys, what's it going to be: martinis or coffee?"

In unison, Cee Jay and Jamie said "Coffee."

"Good. Let's go into the kitchen where we can see what Cee Jay brought in that folder."

When the three of them were seated around the table with their coffee and rolls, Cee Jay opened the file and began to speak. "When Donavon was in law school, one of his favorite classes was Constitutional Law. He was given the assignment to write an argument and present it before the class. He asked me if I would bounce some ideas around with him and check on the writing of the paper. We got together to discuss it on a Friday evening, and by Sunday afternoon, it was finished. He was scheduled to make the moot court speech on Wednesday.

"Apparently Don had a genuine dislike for the Second Amendment. He started by reciting the amendment word-for-word. 'A well-regulated militia, being necessary to the security of a free state, the right of the people to keep and bear arms, shall not be infringed.'

That's it: 27 words and only one sentence long. Since it became effective in 1791, it still remains the shortest amendment and the one that has never been revised or repealed. Don found it hard to believe that it was never repealed. He told me that the Bill of Rights, the first ten amendments, was first proposed in September 1789.

"The new nation was still getting over the Revolution which was fought by private citizens who used their own muskets. There was no army in colonial America; and these minute men, as they were called because they had to be ready quickly to defend themselves and their beliefs against the British red coats, were not issued weapons."

Jamie interrupted Cee Jay. "Yeah I've heard that word 'musket' before, but what the hell is a musket.?"

"It's similar to a rifle today but it had a strap attached to it that a man wore around his shoulders. He literally wore it so that he had it to use all the time. The musket could only fire one shot at a time. Our Founders did not envision more deadly firearms in 1791 The Second Amendment speaks only of the use of arms as 'being necessary to the security of a free state.' It does not mention gaming or sport, although hunting may have been implied because in the 18th century many people may still have been dependent upon hunting for food. Muskets were manufactured and used by armies from 1600 to 1855. So, in the United States we no longer have Minute Men or muskets, but we still have the Second Amendment."

"That's crazy!" Melissa said.

"I suggested that Don do a bit of research about this. He found that muskets or rifles were used as the country moved westward. They were used frequently in frontier battles with the American Indians. The lore of the wild west brought a new type of weapon, the smaller gun, which was not carried around the shoulders but worn around the hips in a holster. How fast you could draw your gun became a quasi- macho thing. Believe it or not, as the West was being settled, the nation lost interest in the Second Amendment and it was seldom referred to for many decades. No one claimed civil rights or second amendment privilege during the Civil War or Reconstruction Era. It was not even an issue connected with the KKK."

"Is that right?" Jamie interjected.

"Surprisingly, it was the National Rifle Association that began using the Second Amendment as a defense for the use of handguns in the United States. Through its members' dues, the NRA is able to lobby members of Congress and politicians in general. That is perhaps the major reason every time there's a mass killing, politicians will call for stricter rules, but ultimately no real changes are made to govern gun use. Gun industry lobbyists have for decades fought against tougher oversight by claiming that gun dealers are among the most heavily regulated businesses in the country. Gun shops do face inspections to ensure they are complying with federal rules, but the ATF or Bureau of Alcohol, Tobacco, Firearms, and Explosives is generally too undermanned and underfinanced to effectively do its job.

"Don discovered that the United States is the only country in the world that does not regulate the use of guns. As a result, the United States has more violent crimes per year than any other country in the world. There are on average 33,000 deaths caused by guns in this country every year. Of this number under 14,000 suicides are by gunshots."

Cee Jay fumbled through pages before he found what he wanted. "Don discovered many statistics to support his case. Just listen to a few. Politicians often claim that gun violence is caused by mentally ill people, yet less than five percent of all gun homicides were done by mentally ill people. But tax monies collected on the sale of liquor and guns are not used for mental health or addiction programs.

"Here is a statistic that drove Don mad: 'The United States has the highest gun ownership per capita of any country in the world. There are 112.6 guns per 100 people, thus there are more guns than people.'

"You may find this fact interesting: There are currently ten companies in the US manufacturing guns. It is currently a $3 billion dollar-a-year industry. Not only does NRA, but also the gun lobby itself, contribute successfully in controlling elections in order to stay in business.

"Here's another that I thought was provocative: 'Since 1968 more Americans have died due to guns than in all three wars we fought in the same period, including Vietnam.'

"Unfortunately, Donavon did not, it seems, pay attention to his own writing. In his paper he stated that studies clearly indicate that gun possession for personal protection is not effective because: First, the average person doesn't always have the gun when it is really needed for that purpose, Second, The gun owner may become nervous in a crime situation and not shot accurately at the criminal, thus injuring innocent bystanders. Third, Instructions are rarely given.

"At first, Don wanted to argue that the entire Second Amendment should be repealed, but I talked him out of that position. I feel that for Americans to repeal it, they would want to replace it with newer and better wording that strongly sets the guidelines for what can and cannot be accepted. Gun ownership is too embedded in our mores. It has become an integral part of who we are. We need a new Second Amendment."

"Like what?" Melissa said. "What do you replace it with?"

"Well," Cee Jay answered, "We spent a lot of time writing and rewriting what we thought would be acceptable to most Americans, and this is what we finalized. I'll read it slowly so you can carefully consider each word.

"The right of citizens to possess firearms for the purpose of hunting, gaming, self-protection and sport shall not be infringed. All states will have the same licensing, registration, and sales of such firearms. The manufacturing, sale, and possession of automatic weapons and firearms greater than thirty calibers and five-round magazines shall be prohibited. Immediately upon ratification, the President shall appoint a special commission of persons to formulate federal rules for the licensing, registration, and sales. All provisions of this Amendment shall take effect one year from ratification."

"Wow! That's quite explicit," Jamie said.

"Don's presentation was lauded by the class and the teacher, but it never went beyond the classroom. You know that is one of the reasons I hope and pray for Don's full recovery and that he does run for the House. If he gets elected, I bet this would be one of his first bills. If anyone can get it done, I think Donavon Rice can do it."

"I just want him to survive, be healthy and happy," Melissa said.

"Cee Jay," do you think Don may really have a future in politics?" Jamie asked.

"Yes, I do. I am convinced America needs a man like him now. One or two terms in the House and one in the Senate and Don can make it to the White House. He has the youthful vitality, good looks, intelligence, leadership style, and charisma to be the next John F. Kennedy."

"Yes, but Kennedy was assassinated," Melissa interjected. "God, forbid that should happen. Don's been through enough with this crazy shooting."

"Don's getting shot just may help him get elected. He may become the poster boy against gun violence. Americans like their presidents to be war heroes. Remember what **PT 109** and **Profiles in Courage** did for Kennedy."

"Yes," Melissa came back, "But Kennedy wasn't gay!"

There was silence for a moment before Cee Jae responded. "Ma dear Melissa Roberts," Cee Jay said with a southern accent, "are you suggesting that Robert Roberts isn't as good-looking as Jacqueline Kennedy?"

The three of them chuckled, then started to laugh, and laugh again, and then started to cry, and then collapsed into one another's arms. Emotions were at a breaking point. "Thank you, Cee Jay. I needed that," Melissa said wiping her tears away.

Chapter 3

------------◆◆◆◆◆------------

Greg was right. Robbie was back in Arizona the next day. His company was able to assign his place to a native Jamaican, and Robbie managed to get on an early flight to JFK in New York and then connected with one directly into Sky Harbor, Phoenix. Before leaving New York, he called Jamie and Melissa with all the details of his arrival.

Robbie's flight was due to arrive at Terminal 4 at 7:20 pm. Melissa and Cee Jay opted to drive up to the airport with Jamie, and to "play it safe," as she said, they decided to leave Desert Lakes at 5:00. "We'll catch the end of the rush hour traffic, and you can never tell about route 10; a small accident can pile up traffic for hours," Melissa said. "I prefer to wait at the airport rather than have Robbie worry about us. And do you guys know how to get around that airport?"

Fortunately, they had little trouble getting to Terminal 4, parking the SUV, and locating the gate; however, because of heavy traffic in the air over Phoenix, Robbie's flight was a half-hour late in arriving and it took another half-hour for the plane to taxi into the gate. Melissa was on edge. It didn't help that Cee Jay went on- and- on about "How God damn fucked up the U.S. air system was."

When Robbie finally came through the gate, his family almost cheered; but Robbie was a mess. He looked as though he hadn't changed his clothes and didn't shave in a week. He had not combed his hair. His eyes were bloodshot from lack of sleep and crying. He looked dazed and confused. The three of them tried hugging him at once. Jamie noticed that his breath was a combination of a lot of stale coffee and too many martinis. He was carrying a duffel bag just big enough to fill an overhead compartment, which Cee Jay immediately took from him.

As Cee Jay led the group quickly to the exit doors and Jamie's car,

Melissa kept a steady stream of inane questions that any mother would ask: *How was your flight, honey? Was the airplane filled? Did you have dinner? Were you able to get any sleep on the airplane?* Jamie was too lost in his own thoughts to pay any attention to her questions or any answers that his son gave her. While he did not actually say it out loud, he wanted to shout at her, *God damn it, woman! He just learned that his husband may be dying. Leave the kid alone!*

All remained silent, as Jamie navigated the way out of Sky Harbor and onto Interstate 10. Ultimately, Robbie spoke. "I called the hospital before I boarded at JFK. They told me that Don's condition hadn't changed and that he was still in intensive care. They told me that I could see him whenever I got to Casa Grande, but only for no more than fifteen minutes at a time."

"Would you mind going directly there before going to Desert Lakes?"

"No problem, son," Jamie immediately responded. "The hospital is right off the highway, so it's on our way."

"We know how much you want to be at Don's side, honey." Melissa turned around and patted his knee.

Robbie was crying. "Mom, I love him so much. I can't imagine living without him." He was still sobbing. "I once told him that I wanted to die before him. He could endure loss, I can't."

Cee Jay moved closer and embraced him. "Love sometimes hurts, Robbie. It's God's way of testing us. That's why when you got married, you said those words to one another. Remember them: "For better or worse, in sickness and in health, in wealth and poverty, until death do you part."

Robbie was still sniffling. "But, I want to be with him forever! You know, Cee Jay, all the hours, days, years with him seem like a moment now. From the day we meet at that ski resort, my entire life has revolved around Don. I am part of him and he is part of me."

Jamie spoke next. "You are very lucky to have one another as part of your lives, Robbie. Hell, look at your mother and Cee Jay. It's love, Robbie, God's love. That's what has kept your mother by my side. And it's what has kept Cee Jay and me together all these years also. Yes, true love! As Cee Jay just reminded us "Until death do you part." He paused momentarily. "But let's not talk about death now. Don's going to pull through this. Just pray for him, be strong for him, encourage him to get well to continue God's work of making us all happy and better human beings.

"Amen to that," Melissa said as they arrived at the hospital.

They entered through the main reception area where they got instructions to the intensive care unit. "Only Robert will be able to visit Mr. Rice," the receptionist told them, "but there is a comfortable waiting room with vending machines and television."

The elevator door opened into the waiting area for the Intensive Care Unit. They found a corner that had three empty chairs, and Robbie went directly to the other side of the area where there were two large doors opening to a wide hall. A nurse sat at attention at a desk in the middle of the entrance to the hall. They could see that Robbie was talking to this nurse. He leaned on the desk to sign something; the nurse gave him a face mask which he seemed to fumble with, and then he disappeared off to the left. From where they sat, it appeared that there were three rooms on each side of the hall. Jamie quickly assumed that all of the patients were being visited because other than the three of them, the room was occupied by one couple that sat together and four individuals who sat alone. No one in this room paid attention to the Home and Garden program on the television screen.

Melissa and Cee Jay were talking about how distraught Robbie appeared. "Under the circumstances, he seems to be holding up, though,"

Cee Jay commented. "I've never seen Robbie like this before."

The minutes ticked by agonizingly slowly. Soon, they took the silent posture of the others in the room, heads were bowed and fists were locked in laps. All one could think of was the six patients in those rooms. Cee Jay wondered how many of them would not come out alive or in what debilitating condition they would be in for as long as they remained alive. *This place is God's waiting room*, he thought. *In another part of this building new lives are beginning, but here is death. Everything we call life comes in between. The irony of it all!*

"Let's get out of here," Robbie said going to his mother. Melissa stood and took him into her arms. Cee Jay went immediately for the elevator button. Jamie patted his son on the back and gently indicated that the elevator was there.

The four remained silent until they were off the hospital grounds and back on the Interstate heading south. "Do you think Don knew you were there?" Melissa asked at last.

"I don't know, mom." He started to cry again. "I wanted so desperately to kiss him. To hold his hand. To see some sign he was alive. His face was covered with a respiration mask so I could not kiss him. There were wires and tubes and machines all around. His right arm was all bandaged up and his left arm was tied down; it looked like he was getting a transfusion. The nurse told me he was getting food intravenously. I think the thing attached to his chest was a heart monitor, and he was also hooked up to a catheter and a bag." He was profusely sobbing at this point. "He looked so still, so innocent. All I could do was tell him over and over that, I loved him and wanted him to go home as soon as possible.

"I asked the nurse if he had shown any sign of being aware. She must have been trying to be funny. She said, "Honey, Mr. Rice is an excellent patient. He doesn't sass or complain about anything."

"Before she told me that I would have to leave, she said that the doctor would be in soon and that depending on his evaluation, there was a possibility that Don could be moved to a regular hospital room. I took Don's left hand and spelled out on his palm '*I love you*."

As they entered Desert Lakes, Robbie asked if he could spend the night at his parents' house. "I can't imagine going into our bedroom without Don being there. I need someone nearby tonight."

"Of course, you can stay with us, Robbie. If you want, your father can drive you to your place to get whatever items you may want. You can stay at our house as long as you want."

"Thanks, mom. I'll be okay after tonight. Tomorrow I'll ask Roger Poquette to stay at my house. He will take me to the hospital. Later, we will probably spend the day playing cards and getting drunk."

Roger Poquette and Robbie were friends from grade school and played together on their high school basketball team. After graduation from high school, he worked at the local hardware store until Robbie convinced him to attend college, and Roger also majored in aeronautical engineering. Roger got his flight certifications a year after Robbie.

Roger never married, but when Robbie and Don moved to Desert Lakes, he bought a house there also. Roger and Robbie formed a limited liability corporation, which Don prepared, and purchased an airplane together. They convinced six other young pilots to sell their houses in Lake Mohawk, New Jersey, and purchase homes in Desert Lakes. The private runway was now servicing six turboprops, one jet, and one hot air balloon. The Roberts Corporation not only built their homes, but extra-large garages for their aircraft. Three of the families also wanted separate, high garages that opened in the front as well as the back for their recreational vehicles. Jamie often joked that he became rich because of fly boys.

****

The next day, Roger took Robbie to the hospital and waited fifteen minutes while Robbie visited his comatose lover. Afterward, they both stopped at Jamie and Melissa's house. Melissa commented on how much better Robbie looked after she made him a big breakfast. He had several hours of sleep and was shaved and in clean clothes. Melissa felt that Robbie appeared more relaxed and cheerful. He related to them that he met with Doctor Fernandez who informed him that if all continued well, Donavon would be taken off the critical list and moved into a regular room tomorrow. Robbie gushed over how much he liked Doctor Fernandez and how he thought he was the best possible surgeon for Don.

"He still says it's still too early to know if Don will have full use of his right arm," Robbie said. "But he joked, saying that he was pretty good in sewing my lover back up."

"That's wonderful news," Melissa said. "We can all visit him tomorrow.'

"Mom, the doctor warned me against staying with him for longer periods and advised that until Don is fully cognizant, other than me, he should not have any visitors."

The chatter coming from the kitchen awakened Jamie. The voices were of Melissa, Robbie, and Roger Puckett. Jamie looked at the clock on the bed stand. It read 11:15, much later than it should be he thought. He wiggled his feet into the bedroom slippers and went into the bathroom, gargled with mouth wash, and proceeded to join the others in the kitchen.

"It's about time you decided to join us," Melissa said. "But you could have at least put on a pair of pants."

Jamie went to her first and embraced her. "And good morning to you too, dear." Grinning he turned to the two men. "Robbie has seen me in shorts before, and Roger has seen worse before, I'm sure." He and Roger shook hands. "Good to see you, Roger. I guess you are glad you didn't get to the clubhouse Tuesday night. Has Robbie filled you in on all the gory details?"

"Actually, Mom has been doing that," Robbie said. "When you called me in Jamaica, all I was interested in hearing was Don's condition and my only thought was to get to him as soon as I could. I suspected that it was that crazy son-of-a-bitch Maxwell who shot him, and Maxwell's last words involved calling Don a fucking homo. That bastard should have been killed." Robbie paused. "But by Don. How? I didn't know Don had a gun."

"Well, he did, and he knew how to use it too" Jamie injected. "Am I getting this right? You didn't know that your lover had a gun?"

"No, I didn't. Mom says that no one knew."

"But the police said that it was registered to him," Melissa said.

"It doesn't surprise me too much that he did not tell me," Robbie said. "He probably didn't want to upset me. He knew I hate all weapons and violence, as he did; but after Gabrielle Giffords was shot down in Tucson on January 8, he was very angry."

"Angry... He was going bananas over that incident," Roger interjected. "You know he went down to Tucson for Representative Giffords' memorial. He told me that while President Obama gave an eloquent speech and gave all the usual nonsense about doing something to control guns in this country, Don knew nothing would actually come of it. That's the only time I heard Don say something negative about Obama."

Robbie took a swig of his coffee. "I think it was right after that Don began to talk about his running for the House. He saw that incident of a college student shooting thirteen people, killing six, and seriously injuring the Congresswoman as a sign that something really had to be done about the Second Amendment."

"He told me that Obama only spoke about putting a band-aid on a gashing stab wound that needed a tourniquet," Roger offered. "He called it an assault on our government and said that it was only the beginning."

"Don took it very personally and felt obliged to do something. What's so ironic about all of this is that Don, who wouldn't hurt any of God's creatures and didn't believe in violence, kills someone."

The conversation seemed to end there. Jamie poured a cup of coffee and Robbie and Roger finished their breakfasts. "Robbie, have you had a chance to call Bob Walsh yet?" Jamie asked.

"No, not yet, Dad. I will though when we get back from the hospital."

Bob Walsh had been Donavon's best friend from grade school. Bob, Roger, and Robbie had played on the same high school basketball team, and it was Bob who introduced Don to Robbie. Don was on their high school football team. When Robbie and Don were married, it was Bob Walsh who was Don's "best man." Roger Poquette was Robbie's teammate and best friend throughout high school, and Roger was Robbie's "best man." Roger moved to Desert Lakes with Robbie and Don. He was still single, but Bob married a college sweetheart, still lived in Sussex County, New Jersey, and had three children. Don was the godfather to Bob's two boys.

Roger was sitting on a barstool in the kitchen with a mug of coffee in his hands. In the silence that Robbie's last statement caused in the room, Roger started blowing on his hot coffee before speaking. "Well, Mr. Roberts are you and Dr. Seton going to join Robbie and me for some heavy drinking and cards tonight?"

"You bet! We'll be at Robbie's at about eight. You better have plenty of money because Cee Jay and I will beat your asses at Shanghai as usual."

Chapter 4

❖ ✦ ✦ ✦ ❖

Cee Jay brought the vermouth; Jamie brought the gin; Roger brought a six-pack of Coors; and Robbie had two-thirds of a stale can of chips in the pantry. It was a typical night of cards at the "Casa Donna Roberta."

Don and Robbie made up the name for their new home the day they moved in. It seemed silly at the time, but the name stuck. The entire family and friends continued using it. No one would say "Let's go to Don's house" or "let's visit Robbie" or "let's go to see Robbie and Don." Instead, people would say something like, "What's happening at Casa Donna Roberta tonight?" Even Barbie and Greg's two children referred to it as "Uncles' Casa Donna Roberta" or "the hanger house." They were amused by the fact that their uncles actually lived- or so they thought- at an airport.

Cee Jay had taught Jamie how to play Shanghai; Jamie taught the game to Melissa who played it with Barbie and Robbie, and they taught the card game to anyone they could. Cee Jay had said that he learned it from Diane, a woman he once knew in New York, but said he thought she made it up herself.

After Jamie and Cee Jay finished their two martinis each, and Roger and Robbie had two beers each, Robbie asked Jamie to go into the kitchen with him to "fetch another round for everyone." From past experience, Jamie knew what his son was about to say in the kitchen. Robbie would hug him and in slurred speech tell him how much he loved him for bringing him and Donavon together and how that was the best day of his life, and how much he loved Don, but Robbie didn't do that. In the kitchen, he broke down crying.

"Dad, what'll I do if Don dies? I can't live without him!"

Jamie hugged and kissed his son. "Who said Don is going to die? Didn't the surgeon tell you today that Don is improving?"

"Yes, but I meant ever. If ever Don goes before me."

"All people who love one another have said that, Robbie. I understand how you feel. I too have questioned how I could handle the loss of your mom or Cee Jay, and I bet they have asked the same question themselves. All we can do, Robbie, is love them with our whole mind and heart each and every day." He paused to look into his son's eyes and kiss him again. "Only God can tell when they will leave us to join Him in the great unknown. And no one has heard God's voice calling for Don yet. So, cheer up! I bet this time next week Don will be back and winning quarters from all of us, as usual. Now, let's get back to the teacher and his former student before they die of boredom together in there without us."

Back in the family room Roger and Cee Jay seemed to be in a deep conversation. "So, what have you two been talking about?" Jamie said. "Did you miss us?"

"No. Roger was asking me about what possessed you to move to Arizona and build Desert Lakes. Maybe you should answer that question yourself, Jamie."

Jamie put the drinks on the card table and grabbed a handful of stale potato chips. "Hem…" he seemed in deep thought. "That's an interesting question, Roger. I got to think about that for a minute." He took a big gulp of his martini. "Perhaps I can answer it in two words."

Cee Jay, Robbie, and Roger in unison immediately said, "Donavon Rice!"

Jamie smiled, "Yeah, Don certainly had a great deal of responsibility for bringing us to Arizona, but I was thinking more of Melissa Roberts."

Together, Roger and Cee Jay said "Melissa?" and Robbie said "Mom?"

"Yes, she was, "I guess you could say, the first to give a reason for coming out here," he said as he shuffled and dealt the cards for the fifth hand of the card game.

"How was that, Dad? Actually, I thought that you and Don had to convince her to leave New Jersey."

"Not really, Robbie. Your Mom had been telling me that our house was too big for us after you and Barbie left for college. Then she started to complain about having to climb the stairs to our second floor." He turned to Cee Jay. "I remember you had the same complaint, Cee Jay. You both were saying that you wished you lived in ranch-style houses like those Don and I built at Sussex Estates. Then I started to complain about the cold winters back there that caused my business to slow down and the resulting loss of income. Melissa began to talk about my taking early retirement and moving to Florida,"

Robbie giggled. "I remember you telling her that you hadn't made a million dollars yet and had no thoughts of retiring until you did. You also referred to Florida as the land of mosquitoes, humidity, hurricanes, and fat-assed retirees."

"Yep, that used to shut the ol' wife up. But the thing that really got her stirred up was our last Thanksgiving family get-together in Sussex County. At the table, she complained about all the work she had getting the house ready and preparing the dinner. You and Don were living in Frenchtown and Barbie and Greg had just gotten married and were in Doylestown. Cee Jay, remember while we were having dessert, she said that next year we should all go out to have dinner at some restaurant."

"I do remember that very well," Cee Jay offered. "That's when Donavon and I started planning for all of us to go on vacation to Las Vegas the following year."

"That's right, Cee Jay. It all started with Melissa not wanting to cook another Thanksgiving dinner and our going to Las Vegas."

"I don't understand, Mr. Roberts. What did that Thanksgiving and going to Las Vegas have to do with Desert Lakes, Arizona?" Roger asked. He smiled. "And I was with you guys in Vegas. remember."

"I sure do, Roger," Jamie said laughing. "Now, let's all give Dr. Seton our quarter for winning another hand. It's your turn to shuffled and deal the last hand, Roger. After the game, I'll tell you all about how that trip to Vegas brought us all here."

When the game ended, Cee Jay was $5.25 richer because he won all six hands. The losers of each hand paid a quarter, plus .50 cents per loser to the person with the highest score in the game. Of course, Robbie and Roger accused him of cheating, but the banter was all in good fun. The four men took their drinks and went into the living room to hear the rest of Jamie's story about Las Vegas.

Jamie seemed lost in his memory as he retold the events. He was happy to reminisce, and the men appreciated his thinking back and talking about those days.

"To continue the tale," Jamie began, "I was surprised when Don and Cee Jay both entered my office that late October afternoon. "Wow! What brings the two of you here at the same time? Don, aren't you supposed to be in your Doylestown office or your house in Frenchtown? Is something wrong?"

"No," said Don, "Dad and I wanted to give you something together. It's a present from us to, you, Melissa, and the rest of the family. We insist that you accept it and that you convince Melissa to accept it also." "Okay," I said in a questioning manner. "Seton, what is this big, surprise gift you are giving us?

"This." Cee jay placed a manilla envelope on my desk.

I stared at the envelope, then at Cee Jay and then Don.

"Open it," demanded Don.

I was still totally baffled. "Listen, guys, things are pretty slow right now, but the company is in a fairly good financial situation. I really appreciate your help, but…."

"For god's sake, open the fucking envelope," Cee Jay said.

"With continued trepidation, I did. A cursory glance at the contents seemed to be two airline tickets and a paper that indicated a reservation for a hotel stay at Caesar's Palace in Las Vegas. "What's this all about?"

"It means that you and Mom Roberts are flying from Newark to Las Vegas on Monday, the 22nd of next month, and will stay at Caesar's Palace Hotel for a full week. We will all be there to celebrate your anniversary on the 24th and have dinner at Caesar's for Thanksgiving," Don explained. "Cee Jay, Robbie and I, Barb and Greg are all going. We have our tickets and reservations. Even Roger Poquette said he might fly to Vegas with us if he can get the time off."

I was speechless and told them so.

"Well, that's a first!" Cee Jay exclaimed. "Jamie Roberts speechless. I never thought that Jamie could be speechless." Then he added, "And just so you know, we were able to get nice discounts through Robbie."

"Remember last Thanksgiving when Mom Roberts said that she didn't want the job of preparing another Thanksgiving for all of us? That was when Dad Seton and I began to think of taking the gang to someplace special this year; and when Barbie told us that you would be celebrating your anniversary the day before Thanksgiving, we knew it had to be a full vacation, like a second honeymoon. We discussed several places, but when

Robbie said he might be able to make discounted arrangements for Las Vegas and none of us had ever been there, it was finalized."

"Honestly, I'm flabbergasted," I said. I got up and hugged both of you. "Vegas, here we come! I'm going to start packing tonight. Melissa will be super excited." Jamie paused briefly. "You know, we never did have a honeymoon. Melissa was pregnant with Barbie and her parents were really upset; mine didn't give a shit. So, we were married and got kicked out of our homes the same day. We were two crazy teenagers madly in love and actually spent part of our wedding day hitchhiking to New York from South Carolina. We spent the first night of our marriage in sleeping bags on a farm field somewhere in North Carolina."

Jamie smiled thinking about it. Cee Jay got up and hugged him.

"I never knew how bad it was for you back then. I'm so sorry I didn't have more compassion when we met."

"Now you have to convince Melissa to go," Don said.

"Convince her? What's to convince? She'll be happy as a butterfly in spring to go to Vegas."

"Well, we hope so, but we know that she has never been in an airplane and is afraid of flying."

"How well I know about that phobia!" I exclaimed. "Imagine, the mother of a commercial pilot who has never been in an airplane. She's going, even if I have to knock her out and carry her aboard that plane."

"This is really interesting. Well, how did you get her finally to fly?" Roger asked.

"Easy! When I got home, I showed her the plane tickets and reservation. Her response was the usual 'Well, I don' know, Jamie.' I shut her up quickly by giving her one long, very passionate kiss and then leading her up to our bedroom. We had the hottest, longest, most passionate sex I think we had since, with the help of God, we created Robbie. We both must have had about three climaxes."

"Robbie, do you hear this?" Roger sounded shocked. "That's your father talking about your mother. I can't believe this!"

"Oh, that's mild, Roger. You should hear him brag about his doing it with Cee Jay."

"He tells you about that too?" Roger stammered. "Doctor Seton, you…."

"Sure," Cee Jay broke in. "We're not embarrassed to talk about our love lives to Robbie and Don. It kind of instructs them and keeps them on step."

Roger turned to Robbie. "Robbie?" was all he could say.

"Well, anyway, as Melissa and I were putting our clothes back on, I told her once again that I loved her, but if she didn't take this free honeymoon trip with me, I would kill her. She came up to me and

whispered, 'You'll never have to kill me' in my ear." "Unbelievable!" Roger stammered.

"I never discussed it again with her, but I know Robbie, Don, and Barbie also added encouragement to her. Barbie told her how nervous she was getting on the plane to go to Bermuda when she and Greg went on their honeymoon. It was her first time in a commercial plane, but she had been up in small aircraft with Robbie before he got his license and said that the larger planes are smooth and far safer. Barbie told her that before the flight they would go to the airport bar and sip wine until she felt ready to take a space rocket to the moon."

"By the day of the actual trip, Melissa was as excited as we all were. She insisted that Greg and Barbie come to our house in Sussex, New Jersey so that they could drive down to Newark in our car to minimize the possibility of anything going wrong. I think she really wanted to have Barbie's added assurance of flying. Cee Jay would also go with us. Robbie and Don were to meet us at the security check-in at the airport two and a half hours before our departure.

"Thank God, Don was already there when we arrived. That settled her jitters about how big and confusing the airport was. She admitted to him that other than Morristown, where Robbie took his first training classes, she had never been to an international airport like Newark, one of the busiest in the country. She noticed that Robbie wasn't with Don and started asking all the nervous questions:" Jamie mimicked: *Where was he? Was Something wrong? Why isn't he here?*

Barbie mumbled, "Typical Robbie! Screwing things up as usual."

"He'll be here before we depart. He got into Philadelphia late with a flight out of Denver. He called to let me know he would be late and that I should drive up to Newark by myself and he would drive to Newark with Roger. Roger was able to get time off, so he'll be going to Vegas with us. Isn't this exciting, mom? We will all be together for Thanksgiving in

Caesar's Palace, and you don't have to do any cooking? Don't worry about Robbie; he will be here, and if not, he and Roger will catch up with us at the airport in Las Vegas."

'Let's go through Security now and check our luggage," Greg suggested.

"Yes, and then head to the bar nearest our gate," Barbie said grabbing her mother's hand and leading to the Security line.

"Good thinking!" Cee Jay exclaimed.

By the time we all got through security and then checked in our luggage and the extra fees for doing so and getting our boarding passes, we only had a half-hour before they were to start boarding our plane. On the way to the bar, Melissa looked out the window and saw the DC 380 we would be flying on.

"Are we going on a monster plane? Oh, my God, I don't think I…" she said to her daughter.

"Come on, Mom. Let's get you something stronger than wine. We don't have time to sip wine."

"Right, you are, honey! Martinis all around. On me," I remember saying in an effort to sever Melissa's mind from the thought that the big monster of an airplane would soon swallow us or will crash and all of us would be killed.

By the time we all were served and had drinks in our hands we only had a few minutes before we had to be back at our gate. Cee Jay gave a toast and Greg said 'Hear! Hear!' I notice that my brave Melissa practically chugged down her martini, winced, then looked at me and smiled.

We were all assigned seats in row 15, which had three seats on each side of the aisle. I gave my seat to Melissa, who wanted to look out the window, I sat in the middle and Cee Jay had the aisle. Greg had a window seat. Barbie, the middle, and Don had the aisle. As we hassled with getting our overhead luggage placed, I heard Don very casually say to Melissa that because Roger wasn't originally sure if he could be with us, Robbie had reserved two seats together elsewhere in the plain. "If I know Robbie, he will wiggle two seats in first-class," he said.

"Too bad that they can't be with us," Melissa said. "Are those tickets just going to be wasted?"

"Oh, no," Don explained. "If they are not here, the airline will offer their seats to stand by customers."

"Typical, Robbie," Barbie mumbled; and Don said, "Be nice, Barbie. That's my husband you're ridiculing."

"Yeah, but he's my brother, so I've known him longer."

The fasten beat belt sign went on, the doors were closed, and it appeared that all 200 seats of our DC 380 were occupied. Melissa saw the men on the tarmac with their batons waving the plane away from the gate. "Well, there's no backing out now," Melissa said. "We're flying to Las Vegas." She grabbed my hand, which she kept tightly for most of the trip.

"Vegas, here we come!" Cee Jay said loud enough for everyone on the plane to hear.

"Weren't we to depart at ten?" Barbie commented almost as loudly. "My watch says it's 10:22 and we're still on the ground."

The plane seemed to creep down one runway, then continued to creep past the terminals before crossing another runway and proceeding slowly down it before coming to a jolting stop. Melissa tightened her grip on my hand. "Is there a mechanical problem with this airplane?

Shouldn't we be taking off?"

Just then we heard a click of the PA system being turned on.

"This is Captain Robert Roberts speaking."

He paused momentarily as if he expected us to drop our mouths, look at one another and say: "What!" Which is exactly what we did.

"Is…is.. Robbie really flying this thing?" Melissa stammered.

"On behalf of co-pilot Roger Poquette and our entire flight crew, I would like to welcome you aboard our DC 380 to Las Vegas." The PA click was heard. The airline insisted that Robbie use his official name of Robert, though most of his colleagues called him Robbie. He pronounced Roger's last name correctly as "poo-kay." The sobriquet Pucket went back to his days in grade school and stayed through high school and even now people thought of him as Roger Pucket," not Poquette. The airline insisted that it be pronounced the way "The" Captain Roberts just did.

The PA click was heard. "Ladies and gentlemen, Captain Roberts here. I have just been informed by the flight tower that because of heavy air traffic in the Newark area, we have been placed in a holding pattern for a few minutes. Any time lost because of delay on the ground, we will try to make up once we are in the air, so our arrival at McCarran in Vegas will probably be on time as scheduled for 1:15, Nevada time. I'll keep the "seat belt light" on until we reach our cruising altitude of 37,500 feet. The flight attendants will be around then to offer you snacks and beverages. Thank you for your patience." The PA clicked off.

After about two minutes, we heard the PA click back on. "This is Captain Roberts again. While we are waiting for the tower to give us the okay to take off, it is my pleasure to tell you about some wonderful people that we have flying with us today. In row fifteen are my mother and father, Jamie and Melissa Roberts. Not only are they going to Las Vegas for Thanksgiving, but they also will be celebrating their fortieth wedding anniversary." He paused briefly, probably anticipating the applause that came from that announcement.

"And with them," he continued, "are my sister Barbie and her husband Doctor Greg Otenburg. Also with them is our dear family friend of many years, Doctor Charles John Seton. Finally, but not the least of this group of very special people, is my husband, Donavon Rice.

"Co-pilot Roger Poquette, who is also a dear family friend, will be sending row fifteen a magnum of champagne with his compliments later. Oh, and one more thing, ladies and gentlemen, my Mom will not appreciate my telling you this, but this is the first time she has ever been in an airplane. I don't know how you helped her overcome her phobia, Dad; but you did, and thanks for that. Mom, I promise you a great flight!" As the passengers clapped, the PA was turned off, and the aircraft slowly began to move again.

When it stopped, the PA was turned on. "Ladies and gentlemen, we just got word from the Newark Tower that we are number three in the queue for takeoff. So, relax and enjoy your flight. You may follow our flight plan on the map on page 32 of our magazine in the compartment in front of you."

Cee Jay broke Jamie's reverie. "You tell a good story, Jamie, but you really haven't answered Roger's question of how and why you built Desert Lakes."

"Well, every story has a beginning, and I just gave you the beginning. Be patient. I know it's late and we are all tired. Tune in again tomorrow over lunch after Robbie and Roger return from the hospital, and I'll continue the tale."

"Fair enough, Mr. Roberts. Man, you have a great memory," Roger said.

Chapter 5

⋅✦✦✦✦✦⋅

The next day Robbie called from the hospital to ask Melissa if he and Roger could stop by for lunch. He said that he would give us an update on Don's status. He also said that Roger wanted to hear the rest of Jamie's story before he had to leave for an assignment the following day.

"Of course, you can, honey," Mellissa said. "Cee Jay and your dad are in the casita getting it ready for Barbie. She called this morning to let us know that she and the two kids are flying out tomorrow. What's this about your dad telling Roger a story? I hope it's not pornographic."

Robbie chuckled. "No. Roger wanted to know the full story of how Don and Dad started Desert Lakes. But Dad had to tell the whole story. You know how he likes to go on and on. Well, last night after the card game, he got as far as the story of my surprising you by piloting the plane to Las Vegas for your anniversary and Thanksgiving."

"But what does that have to do with the Desert Lakes project?" "That's what we all want to hear. See you in about twenty minutes. Love you, Mom. Goodbye."

Melissa went out to the casita, which was to the left of their back patio to tell the men that Robbie and Roger would be there shortly for lunch. Jamie was changing the bed sheets in the main bedroom, while Cee Jay was vacuuming the rug, As she was leaving to go back into the kitchen to make a salad, she said, "By the way, Jamie, Roger says he wants to hear the rest of the story from last night."

Robbie was happy to relate the latest condition of Don. He had been moved into a private room in the hospital and the respirator had been removed. "Mom, he looked so pale. There was no color to his face. His right arm was in a cast, and there were still all kinds of wires hooking him up to a lot of machines and bags in the room. The nurse told me that he was breathing normally and his heart was functioning well. He was still in a comatose state, she said; but when I held his hand, I swear he tightened his own hand on mine and he seemed to be trying to smile. He did not speak or open his eyes, but I did feel that he knew I was with him."

"That's great!" Cee Jay exclaimed. "Did the nurse give you an idea when any of us could visit?"

"No, but she did say that starting tomorrow, I could stay a bit longer than fifteen minutes, particularly if he seems more responsive to my presence."

While they were having their ice cream dessert, Roger turned the conversation back to the story of the founding of Desert Lakes. "What happened in Las Vegas that relates to you building Desert Lakes?"

"Well, I guess the biggest thing that happened was that two weeks after we came back, Barbie announced that she was pregnant. She and Greg must have done more than just gamble, dance, and see shows." Jamie smiled and paused before beginning again.

"You all may remember that after we had dinner at Circus, we strolled down the strip and decided to take a guided bus tour of the city. We got to see such places as the Las Vegas Experience, the street shows at Treasure Island and the newly opened Bellagio, and we were given a few minutes to walk around the casinos at New York, New York, and The Luxor. "The man who was our guide gave us a brief but very interesting account of how Vegas got started out in the middle of nowhere less than a hundred years ago. It was only natural that the men who were there to mine silver and work on laying the rails for the railroad, would play cards, gamble, need a place to stay, and have women brought in for their entertainment and sexual pleasures. Then some guy, who like you boys, was a pilot and builder of planes by the name of Howard Hughes started building hotels and investing big bucks in the town. Along with the gambling, came the mafia, and crime, and wedding chapels, and more entertainment.

"Melissa and Barbie were sad to hear that the guide told us that all Elvis's shows for the entire week were sold out. I could care less. The guide talked about other performers who were in town and that we probably could get to see their shows. The only celebrities that I can now remember were Penn and Teller and Neil Diamond.

"What I kept thinking about, however, was how all of this glitz and excitement began because a bunch of love-starved, drunken immigrants who loved gambling turned the desert into a national landmark with the help of crazy entrepreneurs like Howard Hughes.

"Thinking back on it now, Don probably had the same thoughts as I did."

"How was that, Mr. Roberts? Roger asked.

"Well, you may remember that you and Robbie insisted that we all go to Excalibur Tuesday night for the dinner show there. I'm glad we did all go because it was a lot a fun. I remember you, Melissa, yelling and screaming for the good, handsome knight, and you, Cee Jay, toasting for Sir whoever, while Robbie was standing and waving his chicken leg in the air when the dark knight knocked the handsome knight off his horse."

"As we were leaving Excalibur, Don asked me if I would be interested in renting a car with him on Friday to visit another Nevada town called Laughlin, which was nearby. He also suggested that we would probably have time to spend some time in a place called Lake Havasu, which he said was in Arizona. I readily agreed, saying that we had come this far, why not see some nearby places. After a day of playing slot machines in a few casinos, I welcomed the diversion. I did suggest, however, that Don ask around if any of the others would also be interested. As it turned out, Melissa, Barbie, Greg, and Cee Jay wanted to see some shows and walk around the lobbies of the other hotels." Jamie referred to Robbie and Roger. "You two just wanted to play the tables and get drunk. As I recall, you, Roger said you wanted to check out the women because you had to fly back to Newark on Saturday; and you, Robbie, tried teasing Don by wanting to find a place that had male Chippendale dancers."

The next day we got together in my room to celebrate our 35th anniversary. We opened the bottle of champagne which Roger sent to us on the airplane and Cee Jay gave a toast that brought tears to Melissa's eyes when he said that he wished that we could all be present and be as happy for Barbie and Greg's and Robbie and Don's fortieth. "You youngsters have in Melissa and Jamie and, yes, me also, the perfect examples of 'Amour Vincit Omni.' Cee Jay, you ended saying, 'Jamie, Melissa, 'Ad multos annos."

"We men were dressed in our best evening suits and Melissa and Barbie were wearing beautiful gowns. I was feeling extremely happy and proud as we entered the elegant dining room at Caesar's for our sumptuous dinner. I was the king in the palace and my beautiful wife was the queen."

"Ah, Dad, that was really nice that you made us remember that. And thank you also Cee Jay for that toast. Don and I refer to it often, particularly when having a rough go of things. It helps to keep us focused."

"Thanks, Robbie, and you too Jamie for remembering my little speech," Cee Jay said. "Now let's get back to the story."

Jamie continued. "The next day was Thanksgiving. Don always associated Thanksgiving with high school football. You may remember that Don was a quarterback at Mountain Ridge High, so he dragged Robbie and Roger to see the local game. After you got back from the game, we had our Thanksgiving dinner at Caesar's again. At the table, Cee Jay said a little prayer and then asked that we all tell what we were most thankful for. As an example, he started by saying how thankful he was that Divine Providence directed him to Sussex and Mountain Ridge High School where he reconnected with me and eventually all of us.

"Melissa said that she was grateful to all of us for not making her cook this great meal. I said I was grateful for my wonderful wife, Cee Jay who is the best friend a man can ever have, and my having all of you in my family.

"Barbie said that she was very happy that she met and married Greg, but disappointed that Donavon dumped her for her little brother. I think Don was Barbie's, first real crush. As I recall, you Robbie, Don, and you Roger never said anything after that because two waiters came to take our orders.

Later that evening, Barbie suggested that we go to the Stratosphere Hotel, Casino and Tower to see the view from the observation area. Seeing the strip from up there was really thrilling. I tried imaging how this city had grown in a short period of time and the energies and investments that turned the desert into the dazzling spectacle of light that it was. Even you, Robbie, said the view was better than a night landing in a bigger city."

"Yeah," said Roger. "I'll never forget my first landing at night in Newark. It was awesome, but I was too busy concentrating on landing the plane to really enjoy the descent."

"I agree with you on that, Roger; but for me, it was La Guardia in New York. Every time I land a plane at night, I think of observing Vegas from The Stratosphere. Roger, remember how I dared Don to go with us on the roller coaster that surrounds the observation tower. He was too chicken to join us, so we went together. You talk about an exciting, once in a lifetime experience, that ride had to beat everything."

"That's probably because you and I are pilots and don't mind seeing the world from a different point of view," Roger stated.

"So, the next morning," Jamie continued, "Don and I rented a vehicle and set out for Laughlin. Actually, Laughlin isn't that far from Vegas, and in some ways, it is very much like Vegas, but smaller. Most of the hotel-casinos are on the Nevada side of the Colorado River which separates it from Arizona.

"The first large building in Laughlin is the Riverside Hotel and Casino and it was built, yes, you guessed it, a man by the name of Laughlin. We parked our red mustang convertible, rented vehicle- Don was crazy for red convertibles. As we entered the casino, we could hear the usual noise of slot machines, winners and the occasional cheers of a big winner. We headed to one of the two gift shops in the hotel. I was browsing the postcards while Don perused the books and magazines looking for something on the history of Laughlin and its founder. When he found one, he purchased it and suggested that we go to one of the hotel/casino's seven restaurants for brunch.

"While we were waiting for our meals to arrive, Don started skimming through the booklet that he purchased and began to relate to me some of the information which he found interesting." "Such as?" Robbie asked.

"Well, for starters, he found out that Laughlin's first name was Don, same as his. And Don Laughlin had his own, private airplane, just like you guys. Laughlin was originally from Minnesota, but in 1954 opened a small club and restaurant in Vegas. Ten years later, while flying in his plane, he discovered a barren stretch of rugged desert where the three states of Nevada, Arizona, and California meet at the Colorado River. He was a true enterprising visionary who not only saw the beauty in the place but also its tremendous business possibilities. After doing some research, in 1966 he bought six barren acres and a boarded-up eight-room motel that was in bankruptcy for $35,000 and obtained a mortgage of $200,000. Imagine! ...Six acres of riverfront property for $35, 000 and a mortgage of $200,000. In my book, that's not a deal. It's a gambler's steal."

He and his family lived in four of the eight motel rooms and rented out the other four. That same year, 1966, he built the Riverside Resort which offered all-you-can-eat chicken dinners for 98 cents. It also had 12 slot machines and two gaming tables.

"While we were eating, Don continued to enthusiastically cite other facts from his brochure. He read that Laughlin continued to expand his resort. Today the resort has over 1,350 hotel rooms in two highrise towers. In addition to the casino, the hotel houses a six-plex movie theater, and get this … a huge dance floor for nightly karaoke. Cee Jay would love this place!" Jamie continued. "The hotel also has a 34-lane bowling center, a celebrity theater that seats 800 for top-notch entertainment. It also has a fitness center, two swimming pools, two gift shops, and seven restaurants. It's amazing when you think about it. From a bankrupt eight-room boarded motel in 1966, Don Laughlin's Resort now has 2,000 employees and an annual payroll of well over $40 million."

"Only in America can a man with ingenuity like Laughlin's go from rags to become super-rich," Cee Jay said.

"A lot like you, huh, Dad."

Jamie laughed. "Well, son, I may be well off, but my wealth can't even begin to compare with Don Laughlin's; but Laughlin put a lot back into the community. Laughlin used his money to create jobs and opportunities for others. It takes money to make money; and let's remember that a lot of the ingenuity that Roberts Development utilized came from your husband, Robbie: Donavon Rice.

"After our rather quick tour of the Riverside, we got back in the car to drive up the strip to get an idea of some of the other hotel/casinos. All of them are facing the river and many of them are connected by a walkway so that you can actually walk along the river from one hotel to the next."

Robbie asked if Laughlin operated any other hotels in the town.

"No, just the Riverside. Remember he only had six acres of land. I think he did eventually acquire more acres across the street, however. The Riverside is the only family-owned and operated one in Laughlin. All the others are operated by conglomerate corporations."

Lake Havasu was about an hour-and-a-half drive from Laughlin. I'm glad that Don suggested we go there because we got some good ideas there which we eventually used, or avoided using, in the Desert Lakes project."

"I'm curious," Roger said. "How did Laughlin market his hotel and casino to attract people away from Vegas to his property in the middle of nowhere?"

"That's a very good question, Roger," Jamie said. "Donavon and I talked about that all the way to Havasu. Laughlin used some clever marketing tools- some people may call them gimmicks- but some of them, we later incorporated into our marketing strategies for Desert Lakes. As you may know, Barbie, also helped a great deal with our marketing plans."

"Can you be more specific?" Roger asked.

"Sure. Laughlin realized that most of his customers would be coming from Arizona and California, so the first thing he did was to have the roads improved. Laughlin funded and built the Laughlin Bridge at a cost of $3,5 million. He then donated the bridge to Arizona and Nevada. He also helped fund the improvements at the airport that is just across the river. As you guys probably know, the runway at Bullhead City can now accommodate your Boeing 737 jets. He built a wharf and provided free ferry service from the airport to The Riverside. He initiated a free bus service from Lake Havasu to the casino. He also ran large advertisements in the paper in both Tucson and Phoenix offering very low- cost two and three-night hotel stays with free airplane trips."

"Fascinating!" Cee Jay exclaimed. "So, what did Donavon take you to Lake Havasu to learn other than the fact that college kids have turned Lake Havasu into America's Spring Break capital?"

"Plenty! Like Laughlin, Lake Havasu City was the creation of one very enterprising man, Robert McCulloch. The big difference between Laughlin and McCulloch, however, was that McCulloch already was a very wealthy man. He had inherited a fortune from his grandfather who had worked for Thomas Edison, building his power plants all over the world. McCulloch went to Stanford University and after graduation started several businesses. One of his companies made engines for the Air Force during the Second World War. When the war ended, he continued making airplane engines but also manufactured chainsaws. McCulloch chainsaws revolutionized gardening and forestry and are known and used throughout the world.

"Do you guys know that McCulloch actually made and started to develop a helicopter for individual use? You guys have your own airplane at your home; if McCulloch's plans became more popular, we would all have helicopters rather than cars to get us around."

"That's a great idea, Robbie. Let's work on that," Roger said.

"Like Don Laughlin, Robert McCulloch discovered Havasu while flying his own airplane. He was flying around the Southwest looking for a new site to build one of his manufacturing plants.

"During the Second World War, that area was nothing but a barren wasteland. The Army Air Corps used a small section of it as a base, but when the war ended and the Hover and Parker Dams were completed, the worker's camps moved out. Amazingly, the area remained barren until 1958 when McCulloch bought 3,353 acres from the government. Four years later, after a lot of research and planning, McCulloch acquired another 13,000 acres of federal-owned land in the surrounding area. As recently as September 30, 1963, Mohave County approved the plans for irrigation and drainage, and McCulloch was set to begin selling lots to build his new city. Within fifteen years, the area was sold off, homes were built, and the City of Lake Havasu was incorporated in 1978."

"Why was McCulloch able to buy so much land from the government so cheaply?" Cee Jay asked. "I would think that other investors were vying for land on the Colorado River."

"Probably because of the climate more than anything. Remember this was all part of the Mohave Desert: hot, dry, and barren. The nearest towns were Parker about 50 miles south and bullhead City about sixty miles north. The average daytime temperature is in the 120s and can reach as high as 128. Even in the winter months, the temperatures range in the high 80's to low '90s. That Friday when Don and I went there it was 88 degrees. Nice, but remember this was in November, which is traditionally a cold month in the rest of the country."

"Wow! Why would anyone want to live in such a hot place?" Roger asked.

"Good question, Roger," Jamie said. He paused for a moment. "Remember that line from the movie *Field of Dreams* where Kevin Costner says, 'Build it and they will come.' From October of 1971, when the London Bridge was rebuilt, to the census of 2020 the population grew close to over 56,000."

"So, are you saying that it was the London Bridge that caused people to move there?" Cee Jay asked.

"Yes and no," Jamie replied. "But it certainly was the greatest land development gimmick imaginable, and McCulloch rightfully has been given the credit for it. Did you know that today Lake Havasu with its London Bridge is the second most visited tourist attraction in Arizona.? Only the Grand Canyon beats it. He bought the bridge from the City of London for $2.5 million; but rebuilding it stone by stone in the desert, cost another seven million. McCulloch then had to dredge underneath the bridge, thus creating a channel. His nine and a half million investment was paid back almost immediately by all the free advertisement he got in both England and in papers throughout the U.S. The bridge was officially dedicated in October of 1971, and it was reported that over 50,000 American and British visitors were on hand. Remember that was in October and the temperature was 89 degrees. That began the biggest rush to buy land in the history of land development."

"But didn't buyers know how hot it can get in a desert in July and August?" Robbie interjected.

"Sure! But many of the first buyers were from England where it is usually chilly, damp, and foggy. In the early stage of development, McCulloch operated a fleet of old airplanes such as the Lockheed Constellation and the Lockheed L-188 Electra to bring in prospective land buyers from all over the country, particularly from places like Wisconsin, Washington, and Minnesota where seniors could buy cheaper land in an ideal, warm, dry climate for their retirement. Around the same time, New York retirees were moving to Florida for the same reasons, but problems in Florida were emerging and some big land developers were heading toward bankruptcy. Californians love boating and they saw great opportunities available in the lake and river."

Today, about half the people who own land in Lake Havasu are known as 'snow birds' because they spend winters in Havasu and go to their home states during the summer months. It's a retiree's dream to own two homes. Don and I both quickly noticed the number of RV's or motor homes around town. Many of the homes were actually built with two-story, large garages designed to house RV's and motorboats as well as regular size garages for cars. We used this same concept here in Desert Lakes."

Jamie smiled. "Of course, Robbie and Roger went a step farther with airplanes."

"That's certainly what got me here," Roger boosted.

"Exactly! You and your buddies were among the first buyers of the houses we built here.

The idea of having your house and a hanger to garage your toy aircraft, and a private runway was a novel idea. I understand it has been duplicated in several areas including southwest New Mexico. Farmers and ranchers particularly love it."

"What else did you and Don learn in Lake Havasu?" Robbie asked.

"At the time we went there, I didn't really know what Donavon's true purpose in taking me to Laughlin or Lake Havasu was. I thought of our trip to Vegas, Laughlin, and Lake Havasu was merely a get-away vacation and sight-seeing adventure. I thought of it then only as a fun adventure, but now I realize Don had other ideas and wanted to introduce them to me gradually.

"Don was right in thinking that I would find our trip interesting, but I did not think that he was really laying the groundwork for our next project, which would become much larger than the Sussex Estates project.

"I remember telling Don..... and he agreed.... that McCulloch, who did make a lot of money on Lake Havasu, could have made even more money if he had established a secondary corporation to construct the homes and businesses. He certainly would have had more control of the design and construction of the city. He seemed more interested in selling building lots rather than what was built on those lots. As a result, contractors and construction crews from all over quickly saw opportunities and flocked into Lake Havasu.

"Don and I both were surprised to learn that other than hiring C.V. Wood, who designed Disneyland, to lay out the new city's unique road system, Robert McCulloch didn't take a more active role in the city. This resulted in two of the biggest mistakes that were made in the founding of the city."

"What were they?" Roger asked.

"Because the houses were built in a rather haphazard fashion by independent contractors working at different times and different locations, all homes were built with septic tanks in the ground. Image it: the 2000 census showed there were over 23,000 individual homes and all had septic systems. There were no sewers in the city. None! Can you imagine the health problems that could create? Twenty-three thousand houses on an average 75 by 150- foot lot. The city has now realized the problem and is installing a sewer system, but is assessing each homeowner thousands of dollars to hook up to this mandated system and it will take years before it is completed.

"Because of our experience with Sussex Estates, Donavon and I also immediately saw the power lines. The city almost exclusively relies on electric power; and why not, you have the Colorado River and the Parker and Hoover Dams relatively nearby. If you want a beautiful view of the lake, the surrounding hills, and your neighborhood, you don't want a huge power tower or sagging wires in your view. There have been several studies that show that people who live near those power towers are more susceptible to developing cancer. Many citizens told us that they heard a constant humming from the transformers. I don't know how accurate these studies are, but wealthier retirees avoid living near power towers. Just like the sewers being in the ground, electric lines also, for the most part, should be underground to start with, in new developments. Yes, it is more costly, but it is cleaner and safer than the towers.

"Along with power lines, television antenna tend to mar the appearance of neighborhoods. Originally, there were no satellite or cable companies, so if you wanted a clear television picture, you had to put up an antenna that was high enough and strong enough to get a signal from Las Vegas or Phoenix. The city of the future should bury television cables in the ground also. People who are rich enough to buy into a community want it to be aesthetically pleasing, not like the old city landscapes that they are trying to get away from. Don and I were careful about the aesthetics of our communities, even if it cost more. We designed homes specifically with this in mind. Unfortunately, we didn't quite keep up with technology, however, when it came to solar energy. Even in that regard, Tesla and other companies are working to improve the roof appearance of panels. They now have panels that look more like shingles. I've seen some prototypes and it is hard to tell the difference." Jamie paused and lowered his chin into his chest. "But that is coming too late to save asshole idiots like Maxwell."

Robbie walked to his father and both men embraced. Robbie started crying. "I know I shouldn't say this, Dad, but I'm glad Don killed the son-of-a-bitch trouble maker. If Don doesn't pull through this…" He broke down sobbing and could not finish speaking.

Cee Jay then embraced Jamie and Robbie. All three were crying. "Don's going to be okay, Robbie," he said. "We all love him so much. God's going to hear our prayers."

"Amen to that," Jamie said wiping tears from his eyes. Turning to Roger, he said, "I know I haven't told you the full story yet about how Desert Lakes got started, but I promise I will finish the story tomorrow. Let me do some recollecting tonight. Barbie and her two kids are flying out tonight. Tomorrow, after, we know Don's updated condition, I'll finish the story. I want my grandkids to know how their Uncles Robbie and Don Don built a community and how their Grandpop made a fortune that someday they may be proud to inherit."

"So far you've done a marvelous job of reminding all of how it got started, Jamie. Good job!"

"I'll second that, Dr. Seton," Roger said.

"Oh, for god's sake will you stop calling me Dr. Seton. You graduated fifteen years ago, and now just call me Cee Jay. Okay? We are all family here."

The former teacher and student hugged.

Chapter 6

The next morning Jamie woke to the sound of happy children playing. The sound of his grandchildren brought a smile to his face as he rolled over to touch his wife. His hand moved a few times over the sheets before he realized that Melissa was not in bed with him. She was already out of bed and entertaining the children in another part of the house. He rolled over to see what time it was on the nightstand clock. Deciding that 8:30 was late enough for any retired man to stay in bed, Jamie got out of bed, wrapped himself in a bathrobe, and headed in the direction of the kitchen. He and Melissa had been awake late into the night reminiscing and checking details of their memories of the last several years and the construction of Desert Lakes. Jamie wanted to make sure the rest of his story was accurate.

"Pop! Pop!" Greg Junior yelled as soon as Jamie entered the room.

He grabbed his grandfather's hand and lead him into the room. "Mom-Mom is showing us how to make rolls. Wanna help us?"

For a moment, Jamie had an image of Robbie and Barbie as youngsters and Melissa making rolls in their house in Sussex. He loved those memories, but now Barbie was here with her own two children. "Good morning, sleepyhead," Barbie said giving her father a kiss on his cheek. "You're just in time for mom's fresh-baked rolls."

Jamie kissed his wife and then his granddaughter Missy. The table was already set with orange juice glasses, coffee mugs, glasses of milk, marmalade, and other jellies and assortments of buns. As they sat down around the table, Barbie said, "Kids, when your Uncle Robbie and I were children, Mom-Mom and Pop-Pop would always love having Saturday breakfast together like this. Only Mommy and Uncle Robbie were better behaved than you squirmy kids," she added tossing her hand over Greg

Junior's head. "Isn't that right, Dad?"

"Yes, but we always said a pray first and held hands."

"So, let's do that now. Children, hold hands and bow your head before digging in. Dad, say a pray."

Jamie cleared his throat. "We thank you, God, for giving us this day. We thank you for bringing us together to love one another this morning, and we pray that Don recovers well and quickly. Amen."

"What's wrong with Don-Don?" Missy asked. "Uncle Robbie said he was in da hos pit al."

"That's correct," Melissa explained. "Uncle Don was very seriously hurt in an accident and can't be with us for a while."

"I want to stay at Uncle Robbie and Don Don's house," Greg Junior said.

"Don't you like it here with your grandmom and pop and staying in our casita?" Melissa asked.

"Yes, but it's more fun with Uncles Robbie and Don. They play games with us and give us candy and stuff."

"Hem," Jamie replied. "Didn't anyone ever tell you to be careful around men who played with you and gave you candy?"

"Yes, but daddy said that about you, Pop-Pop and Uncle Cee Jay. Not Uncles Robbie and Don-Don."

Jamie chuckled. "I'll have to tell Cee Jay to stop giving you guys candy."

"He never does," Missy chimed. "And he never makes us laugh like Uncles Don-Don and Robbie do."

"Speaking of Robbie, is he coming here this morning?"

"He called me earlier," Barbie said. "He is going to the hospital first, but he and Roger will be here this afternoon. He told me that Roger and he wanted to hear the end of your story about building Desert Lakes before Roger has to leave. Robbie said he was driving him down to Tucson for a seven o'clock flight."

"Ah, yes! The end of my story. Well, it's really Don's story as much as it is mine because, without Don, it would never have happened. I particularly want you kids to hear the story, so you have to promise me that you will behave and listen carefully to Pop-Pop and Uncle Don- Don's story of how we came to live in Arizona."

"I promise," Greg Junior said. "As long as Missy promises not to giggle."

"I promise too," Missy said. "But I do not giggle! It's Junior who makes me laugh."

"Well, that's what little brothers always do," Barbie said. "They put a smile on their big sister's face. It's because they love each other. Isn't that right, mom?"

"That's right, dear. Now I want you children to sit still later while your grandfather tells us his story. Promise?"

"Yeah, we'll be good," they said in unison.

Several hours later, Robbie and Roger came in time for lunch. Earlier they had been to the hospital. They were met in the driveway by Jamie, Melissa, Barbie, and the children who had all been outside admiring the blooms on one of Melissa's recently planted prickly pear cacti.

Robbie immediately hugged his sister and bent to kiss Missy and Greg Junior while Barbie and Roger warmly shook hands.

"How is Don this morning?" Melissa asked.

There was a pause as Robbie looked at his mother, then at Roger with a solemn gaze as though he were looking at Roger to help him answer the question. "Better, I think," he finally said.

"I still was not permitted in the room," Roger offered.

"And the nurse suggested that I leave after being there for only fifteen minutes. She said something about having to administer another injection which would put him to sleep. He did open his eyes and I could tell that he knew it was me. He seemed to smile when I held his hand." Jamie asked if he was able to speak.

"No. He still is wearing the ventilator mask."

"I thought they had taken that off yesterday," Jamie said.

"Yes, Dad, they had. But he had it on again today. That's what worries me. As I was leaving, I asked the nurse about that. She said that she was following the doctor's orders, but didn't know why the doctor ordered more oxygen again. And no visitors permitted yet...."

Barbie embraced her brother. "Don's going to make it, Robbie. Don't worry. He's a fighter and no bullet is going to stop him. His love for you and his causes are too great."

Missy grabbed her uncle's leg. "I love Uncle Don-Don," she said.

"Well, let's go inside," Melissa said. "You boys look as though you could go for some White Castle cheeseburgers."

"Your mom is a mind reader, Roberts," Roger said as they headed into the house. Turning to Jamie, he asked if he was ready to finish his story.

"Sure am, Roger. I even wrote out some notes to keep me on track."

"I hope so, Mr. Roberts. Keep it short, okay. I have a flight out of

TUS, so Robbie and I have to leave around 4:30." "Roger that, Roger," Jamie said smiling.

Cee Jay came as they were finished their light lunch. Barbie and Malissa stayed in the kitchen to 'clean up and catch up.' Cee Jay challenged Roger to a game of chess in the family room. Robbie and Jamie agreed to play Hide and Seek outside with the children.

Eventually, the children tired of their game, and Jamie said it was time to finish the story just as Roger was telling Cee Jay he had been 'castled.'

"Before you begin," Cee jay said, "may I have a stiff martini, Jamie? That kid just defeated me again, and I need one."

"Ah, Cee Jay just lets me win because it makes him feel generous." "Now, we could all stand a stiff one," Barbie announced sarcastically.

"Gather round, kids," Jamie said walking over to the bar. "Cee Jay and I will be your bartenders before you settle down to hear the remainder of how we all came to live in Arizona."

After all the adults had their drinks and the children were served Shirley Temples by their Uncle Robbie, they scattered about the room to listen to Jamie, who settled on a barstool in front of the bar. Malissa sat next to Robbie on the love seat. Cee Jay and Roger sat at the chairs at the chess table. Barbie positioned herself on the floor with the children on each side.

"Let's see," Jamie began, "yesterday I told you about the side trip from Vegas that Don and I had to Laughlin and Lake Havasu. That was in November. Let's skip ahead now four months to the end of March.

"I was at my desk in the Sussex office when Don showed up unannounced late one afternoon. "Don,' I said surprised, 'what brings you to Sussex? Last time you were here, you and Cee Jay gave me plane tickets for Vegas."

"After shaking my hand warmly, Don said, 'I came to give my best father-in-law another present.' He handed me a big envelope.

"So, this time you're sending me to Disneyland?"

'No,' Don said. 'You and I are going to Phoenix, Arizona, and then a place called Casa Grande.'

"What's in Casa Grande? Is Disney opening a new park there?"

Don smiled. "No, dad. Casa Grande is a short distance from Phoenix. We will be staying at the Holiday Inn there for a few days while we explore the Sonoran Desert nearby in our four-wheel-drive Jeep." He dropped the keys on my desk.

"Yep, Roberts, LLC now owns a brand-new company car."

"What the hell do I need a jeep to get to Sussex Estates?"

"I'm not talking about Sussex Estates, Dad. I got it for some pretty rough terrain over desert and cotton fields in Arizona, and you and I may be needing a jeep soon"

"I smell another project is on your mind, Don. But why Arizona? Are you comparing me to a Don Laughlin or Robert McColloch?"

"Well, nothing on that kind of scale, but yes. A new landdevelopment project for our corporation to expand west."

"Why, Arizona?"

"Robbie has been flying to Phoenix a lot lately and Roger has been in and out of Tucson. They both tell me that other than Casa Grande there is almost nothing between Phoenix and Tucson but desert and open range and a few cotton fields. I didn't know this about Arizona, but it once was a leading producer of cotton, but now that industry is rapidly fading. Robbie and Roger both feel the population of Arizona is rapidly growing and now may be the time for us to get land while it is still relatively cheap. Let's face it, Dad, we need growth and Arizona just may be the place to develop your retirement project."

Jamie smiled and thought for a while before speaking. "Okay, Don. How soon before I get to ride in our new corporate limousine?" "Open the envelope," Don said.

Inside the envelope, I found two round-trip airline tickets and a hotel reservation for a four-night stay. They were dated for March 22 departure from Newark and a return on Friday, the 26th.

"You do realize that March 22 is next week, don't you?" Jamie said. "That doesn't give us much time to get ready, and I'll have to run this whole thing through Melissa."

"Robbie and I have already done that, and she is okay with it. She really likes the idea of a move to Arizona."

"And what about Cee Jay. I can't leave him here in Jersey."

"I spoke to him this morning about the concept. He wants to take early retirement from Mountain Ridge and this project may force him to have a change of scenery. He said that he would buy the first house we put up."

"It looks like you have touched all basis with the family on this, Don." Jamie smiled and added, "I guess I should start packing. McCulloch and Laughlin had their private planes for exploring the land. All I'll have is a four-wheel-drive jeep."

Jamie continued his account.

So, the following week Don and I found ourselves in Phoenix. Just outside the airport, we found our new jeep. Thank God Don seemed to know how to drive the damn thing because I couldn't handle the traffic getting out of that airport and the jeep at the same time. Navigating the traffic on the Interstate, which is just outside Sky Harbor was a challenge itself. Once we were clear of the Phoenix area, it was clear sailing down to Florence Boulevard at Casa Grande. That was the first time I saw the hospital on our right and a Fry's grocery store on our left. We checked into our room at the Holiday Inn.

"Looks like you and I are finally going to be in bed together, dad," Don commented, sitting on the edge of our king-size bed.

I remember telling him to Shush I wouldn't tell you, Robbie, about that little fact, but we didn't do a thing that you should care about anyway. We had dinner at the hotel, had a few drinks at the bar, and then spent that night in our room talking about the research Don had done about the area.

He had a map of Arizona and pointed out to me the interstate 10 between Phoenix and Tucson. Other than Casa Grande, there were no towns between the two major cities. Off to left was the small town of Eloy and north of Eloy was Coolidge. It was the land between these two small towns and Route 10 and Route 79 that interested Don. He had checked with Pinal County and there was abandoned land that the County had tried to auction without success. He also checked with a realtor in Casa Grande about land for sale in the area. He found out that the shopping and entertainment area across the highway was just recently developed. The realtor gave him a listing that he had for 640 acres that had been cotton fields. The seller was retiring, and the land was going to waste. The asking price, which included a three-bedroom and two-bath house as well as a large storage barn was $540,000. By New Jersey standards that would be called "a steal." The realtor never mentioned it, but Don had noticed that the realtor's commission was contracted at 10% and that the listing had actually expired a little more than two weeks ago.

Don felt that if we could negotiate the property for under a halfmillion and acquire some of the County property, we would have an ideal setting for a new housing development. The location, between two major metropolises - Tucson and Phoenix, was really great; and the proximity to Casa Grande could supply a new community with entertainment, food, and medical needs, while the nearby town of Eloy would welcome building projects for its skilled construction workers.

Don called the owner of the acreage that was being sold, Mr. Herb Wolf, and asked him if he would be available the next afternoon. Mr. Wolf seemed more than happy to show us around the property; he also gave clear directions to get to his house.

We set out early the next morning with enthusiasm. Don's excitement for this project had made me eager to explore the possibilities. We headed south back on Interstate 10, but just a short distance down we saw a sign for an exit that pointed to "Arizona City and Sunland Gin Road." Don said that he wanted to check this community out because you, Robbie, knew a pilot that lived there.

"Yeah," Robbie said. "Roger and I both know Curt Manning. Curt bought there because it was close for him to both Sky Harbor and TUS, but said that he and his wife hated living there."

"Curt said Arizona City sucked," Roger added.

"Well, you guys got Curt to be one of the first buyers here in Desert Lakes a year later," Jamie continued.

Curt was right when he said the town sucked, but it taught Don and I a few things not to do here.

The community is several miles down Sunland Gin Road from the interstate.

Jamie smiled. You know I really like that name. There is plenty of land drenched in sun, and I like my gin. We stopped at a building that was called the "Arizona City Home Owners' Association and Community

Center" and went inside. A woman working at the only desk in the room stood and greeted us at a counter. She introduced herself as Cindy, the president of the HOA. Don introduced us and told her that we were visiting from New Jersey and wanted to learn about the communities in the area.

Cindy was very accommodating. She told us that she lived in Arizona City for five years and that she and her husband lived on "the lake" in a house that her husband, a construction contractor, had built himself.

Don quickly pointed out that she said "the lake." "There is a lake out here?" he asked.

"No. It's more like a man-made pond that the developer dredged out and filled with irrigation water. In the center, it has colored lights around a pump that used to shoot water ten feet into the air. You could actually see it at night from the Interstate, but the pump broke about two years ago, and the association doesn't have the money for a new one. The lights and fountain as well as the "lake" itself were a landmark that actually drew people here and sold property. That is until the developer flew the coop and left the community stranded for any real development."

Don and I looked at one another and nodded. We had learned our first lesson in marketing. We also learned that the developer, like McColloch in Lake Havasu, was only interested in selling lots rather than in building homes and community. This helped Cindy's husband for a short while, but then other contractors moved in, competition caused building to be more concerned with cost than quality, and eventually new buyers disappeared.

She opened the double doors to show us the community hall. The developer built this building, but left it up to the Association to maintain as well as everything else in the community," she said. "Our only source of income is a small profit we make by renting the hall to an Evangelistic preacher for Sunday morning services. We also run a bingo here every Wednesday night during the winter months." Don wanted to know more about her HOA.

"Well, because of the way the town was established, we never really had a mandated association. I guess you could say that I took charge and have been trying to get things going, but the people just don't want to pay for an association. People here are very independent and want no part in government or "associations." As a result, Arizona City is not incorporated, and I doubt very much if it ever will be. We do have a volunteer fire department, but no city services. Kids have to be bused to Casa Grande for school, we have to rely on the County for most services such as policing. A few of the residents belong to the sheriff's department. There is a postal substation here. It is privately owned but no mail is delivered.

I guess you gentlemen would consider Arizona City part of the real shoot 'em up wild west"

Don and I again looked at one another and nodded. We had just learned a few new marketing pointers.

"We may be interested in talking to your husband about a building project we are contemplating in the area. Would you give us his name and telephone number?"

"Sure. Bill is always willing to get new jobs. I have his cards right here." She gave each of us a business card. We thanked her and said that we would be in touch. Leaving the building we decided to take a short drive around the community and particularly to see the lake and to check on the impression we had received from the HOA president. She was right. The roads were in bad shape, several were only gravel and a few led to dead ends. There were many building lots haphazardly sitting throughout the community. There was a large mixture of different styles, sizes, and quality homes, which obviously was the result of many different contractors working at different times and locations. We saw no parks or commercial or industrial areas. There were no schools. Eventually, we did find the lake, which was more of a pond. A few homes were built around it but there were more vacant lots filled with bullrushes and cacti than homes. We did see a modern, multi-level, mostly glass home that I immediately guessed was the one that Bill and Cindy built for themselves. In a better market such a home would have been valued at around $400,000, but sitting as it was amid the blight, probably would sell below the cost of building it.

As we headed out of Arizona City and back to the Interstate and our meeting with Herb Wolf and his 640 acres, Don commented, "Boy, Robbie's friend Curt Manning, was right. That town really does suck. Why would anyone want to live there?"

"When Curt and his wife bought their lot and had their house built, the developer probably pictured it a lot different than what it became because of poor planning."

"You can say that again," Don said. "That place is worse than Lake Havasu."

"At least we didn't see any mobile homes or manufactured home parks."

"I'm willing to bet that was because the original developer of Arizona City wrote a deed covenant that restricted them." "What about age restrictions?" I asked.

"Probably not. The majority of potential buyers would be under age 55 who wouldn't care about fancy club houses, pools, or golf courses. They would only be interested in low priced homes and low taxes."

"Yes, but what about kids? Younger couples do tend to have children who need an education."

"They could bus the kids to Casa Grande or Eloy."

"Would you want your kids to ride an hour or so on a school bus each way?"

"Hell, no!"

"So, there's your answer. No age restriction is necessary. If couples want to raise a family, they buy a nice new home now and when the kids get to be school age, they sell at a profit and move on. Or home school."

"Or have the kids ride the bus. After all, with no commerce or jobs available in town, mom and pop have to travel for work, so why not have the kids travel to school?"

"Or they could be like you and Robbie.... Gay with no kids."

"True. But don't count on it. Robbie and I have been talking a little about adopting a child."

"Hem. That sounds good, to me," Jamie said with a smile on his face. He chuckled. "Imagine.... Robbie being a father."

"Why are you laughing?"

"I can picture you being a father; but Robbie.... He's just a kid himself."

"Robbie is 33, dad. And I'm 34. Neither of us are kids and we're not getting any younger. I seem to remember hearing that you were only 17 when Barbie was born and 21 when you had Robbie."

Still smiling, Jamie said, "You got me on that, Don. You two should have kids while you can."

Don reached his hand over to his father-in-law's and held it firmly until he turned off the highway and onto a gravel road leading to Herb Wolf's house.

The road to the house had many ruts that indicated it had not been graded in several years.

"Look at that," Jamie exclaimed pointing to his left. He was referring to a large patch of land that resembled a stagnant pond or swamp surrounded by sage bushes and weeds. The water was black. "I thought this land was once a cotton field. It looks like a swamp to me." "Or a lake," Donavon interjected.

"Shades of Arizona City?"

"Only bigger," Don noted

"This one will need a hell of a lot of dredging to make it a lake."

"Hey, a lake in the middle of the Sonoran Desert."

"That's it! Desert Lakes. Sounds nice." Don smiled. "We could call our new project Desert Lakes."

Jamie thought for a moment. "Sounds a lot better than Arizona City," he said as they approached the house.

Herb was standing on his porch as if waiting for the men to arrive. He waved to them as he walked down the steps from the porch to the road.

"You must be Don and Jamie. I'm Herb Wolf. I'm glad to meet you."

The men stood outside talking for a few minutes. Herb reiterated that the house had three bedrooms, two full baths, and that it had a new metal roof. He waved his arm over the land and said that the sale included 600 acres of cotton fields.

"Are you fellas cotton farmers?" Wolf asked.

Don smiled. "No. I'm Mr. Roberts' attorney. I also happen to be his son-in-law."

"Oh, I see. "So, Jamie, you must be interesting in dairy farming. This is a great area for dairy farming, ya know. I ran it for cotton all my life, but my kids wanted no part of raising cotton and I just can't do it alone. Not at my age."

Jamie spoke. "No. I'm not a rancher, Herb. I'm into construction. I'm thinking of building some houses in this area.

"Ah, I get' cha," Herb said. "You're one of those *de-vel-o-pers*. I gotta warn you, though: there ain't much industry around here except for cows and cotton. People are moving outta Pinal County; not movin' into it."

"Yeah, I know that," Jamie said. "That's why I'm being so careful while looking to get going building 'a few' houses in the county." Jamie deliberately didn't want to give the impression that he was truly interested and well experienced in development. He knew that the best way to negotiate with Herb Wolf was to talk on a level with him.

The men stopped to scan the area from the front porch.

Pointing to the swampy pond, Don asked, "Is that a natural pond over there?"

Herb chuckled. "Well, I guess you can call it that. When my kids was little, they loved divin' and swimmin in it. Now they is adults and have their own private pools in Scottsdale and California. After the wife died, I just kind'a let the pond go to hell. I think there is a spring in rocks on one side of it where the water comes from." Changing the subject quickly, he led Jamie and Don into his house.

Don was immediately impressed by the beamed logs in the ceiling and the large rock fireplace in the living room. Herb showed them through an office and a formal dining room, and a large eat-in kitchen.

The potential buyers were interested and asked several questions concerning plumbing, heating, air conditioning, etc. The house had a septic system and a well. Overhead wires brought in the electricity for the house and storage barn, but there was no central air conditioning. Jamie was surprised to learn that the house was heated by natural gas rather than propane. Mr. Wolf explained that the gas company that served Eloy extended pipes out to his place.

As they toured the house, Don thought that the adobe building was cozy but needed cleaning up and some minor cosmetic improvements. A dishwasher was a must. Jamie thought that he and Melissa could live in it temporarily until they could build their own newer place. It could also serve as an office during early construction.

"Well, fellas, now that you've seen the house, let me take you on a trip around the land," Herb said as he led them to the sliding doors between the master bedroom on one side and the kitchen on the other that lead to a covered patio. "So, what do you think of my house itself?" he asked.

Don was the first to respond. "I really like it very much. I'd like to duplicate the layout in my own home."

Jamie was a bit more cautious in his enthusiasm. "The house seems

solid enough for me, but, of course, my wife would have to see it first."
Herb Wolf led the men to the large barn across from the patio. Except for
his automobile and a jeep, the barn was empty. It was obviously used as a
cotton baling and storage facility at one time. "I'll drive you around the
farm. Hop on, men."

"Is that mesa over there part of your property?" Jamie asked as they
were leaving the barn.

"No, my property ends about 150 feet from here. That rise and the
land around it belongs to the county. The county tried selling it at auction
a few years back. I considered bidding on it myself, but it's too hilly and
rocky for farming. A lot of land around here has caliche which makes it
worthless for dairy or cotton." "What's caliche?" Jamie asked.

"You fellas ain't from Arizona. Caliche is found a lot throughout the
Southwest. It's like cement that mother nature puts in the ground to keep
farmers away from spoiling the landscape. Depending on how deep it is
and how thick, only cactus and snakes will grow on it." "Can you dig a
well through it?" Donavon asked.

"Most well augurs can cut through it, but it really depends on how
thick it is," Herb explained.

He drove over a rough path to the pond and stopped the jeep. Up close
it seemed much larger to them than at first glance. Herb pointed to a tree
on the opposite side. "The kids loved jumping into that pond from a rope
we had on that tree. The water is about six feet deep on that spot." "Is that
the deepest spot?" Don asked.

"I really can't say," Herb responded. "That's the only area I ever
measured. I wanted to make sure it was safe for the kids to jump from the
tree and those rocks over to the left. The spring is somewhere within those
rocks and it creates a kind of waterfall effect as it trickles into the pool. The
pond itself bends with the terrain over to the left. It may be shallower over
there, but the kids did have a raft in that area and used to dive off it and
swim to this section. Come on; let's walk over there to see it."

Looking at the wooden raft which seemed to be collapsing into the
pond, Donavon thought back to his happy days spend at the Culver Lake
boy scout camp and how he and Robbie fell in love while sunning on the
raft there.

"I'm just guessing," Jamie said, "but this whole swamp is about 300 by 225 feet."

"You may be about right," Herb responded. "But with all the silt and growth around it now, it's really hard to tell. I seem to remember it was close to three acres of the total 640 acre here. We'll have to check the original deeds to find out exactly what the acreage is." Herb paused for a moment. "Let's just say it will require some dredging to get it back to its original, beautiful scene here."

"Yes, I can imagine how picturesque it must have been here fifteen or twenty years ago," Donavon commented.

"There something else I want to show you, gentlemen. Shall we?" Herb indicated that the men get back into his jeep.

Driving to the southeast of his house, he soon stopped at what first glance resembled an old road in disarray that hadn't been used in many years. Tall weeds were growing through the cracks in the blacktop. Chucks of tar were mixed with gravel. Jamie thought that it may have been part of a county road that was abandoned.

As they were swinging out of the jeep, Don exclaimed, "Holy shit! This looks like an old runway!"

"You got that right, young man," Herb said. "It is a 5,000 by 30-foot runway. My son David was always interested in model airplanes, and before he was even legally old enough to get a pilot's license, he was flying his own Cessna crop-duster. He convinced me to kind of build this runway. David earned his way through ASU crop dusting and putting on air shows. David got his flight certifications in Venice, Florida. Today he is a commercial airline pilot. He lives in Scottsdale but flies all over Europe and the U.S.A."

"Wow! That is a coincidence because my son is also a commercial pilot. He lives in Pennsylvania but lately has been flying out of Newark, Tucson, and Phoenix. Perhaps my son knows your boy."

"Maybe they do, but I seldom see or hear from David anymore. I wanted him to take over my cotton business and we got into an argument and he kind of went his own way."

"At one point I wanted Robbie to take over my construction business, but all his interests were about airplanes and basketball. Now, my son-in-law

Don is my partner in the business; but fortunately, my son and I are still very close."

"Yeah, I guess no matter how much you love them, you have to let your kids follow their own paths. You see that ransacked building down there on the right. That's the remains of a hanger that David built himself for his old airplane."

"I'll have to ask Robbie if he knows a pilot by the name of David Wolf," Don said. "Really a strange coincidence."

"Well, I'll show you around the fields now. Hop on," Wolf said getting back into his jeep.

The road from there was mostly dirt with large ruts. They headed south to what Herb referred to as the southeast corner of the property. He explained to the men that there were irrigation stations at all four corners of the property which measured one square mile. He explained that in the barn there were four rolling sprinklers that had been used to irrigate the fields at the same time.

"The water pressure's good enough to handle that?" Jamie asked.

"You batcha!" Herb responded.

From the general perimeter, Jamie and Donavon were able to get an overview of the size and condition of the land. They stopped at all four irrigation pump stations on the property, and after checking the one at the far northeast corner, headed back to the main house.

"Well, gentlemen, now that you've seen the whole spread, can I offer you a beer or a pop inside before you head on back to Casa Grande?"

Don spoke for both of them. "We're fine, thank you, Herb. What I guess Jamie and I would like to do though is wander around the property for a while and talk things over, if that's okay with you. Then we will stop by your place again in about an hour to share our ideas with you."

"That sounds okay with me, Don. Do you have any questions for me now?"

"Not right now, Herb," Jamie said; "but if you have a copy of the real estate listing, I'd like to see it again; and by then I sure would appreciate a beer."

"Good enough. I'll meet you men back here soon"

As Jamie got into the side seat, Don gave him a questioning look.

"What?' Jamie said.

"You said you would take him up on that offer of a beer."

"So?"

"Jamie, in all the years I've known you, I have never seen you drink beer."

"Yeah, and probably never will after today. If I make an offer on this land, I want the seller to think I'm one of his kind. You know one of the boys that will level with him and treat him right. Asking for a martini or margarita would just be wrong."

"Dad, you make a great negotiator. You should be a politician."

"Nah. It's just my New York street smarts at play."

"You're a wise man, Jamie Roberts," Don said driving away from the house. "So, I'm guessing you're going to make an offer."

"Maybe. Let's take another look at that swamp. I want to see if water is really coming from those rocks, and where it is going."

Don drove to the pond and then found a way of driving above it so that the rock formation was below them. From there they realized that this was the highest point in the flat surrounding area. They could see the entire property from this point. Donn hopped out of the four-wheeler and started to carefully go down the rocky formation. Jamie followed. Don noticed some moss in the rocks and then felt some moisture. There was water glistening in the sun and falling into the pool.

Jamie found a large rock nearby and sat down to observe Don, the oak tree that years ago was the focus of kids swinging into the pool. He seemed to be in deep thought.

Donavon joined him on the boulder. "What are you thinking, dad?"

"I'm wondering where the water goes from here and why these pools aren't bigger."

"My guess is that it evaporates in the sun and is absorbed by the bushes and weeds. I'll bet that on the other side the water around that raft was a couple of feet higher at one time. We could pump over there to recycle the water to bring it back here as a kind of waterfall." Don stood and moved about the narrow landing.

"Picture it, dad, this natural pool increased by a couple of yards all round. A club house and recreation center on the other side. Maybe we can dig another pond on the north side near where the road leading up to that mesa is."

"The mesa is on county land," Jamie reminded Don.

"You mean the land that you are also going to bid on and build Melissa's dream home on."

"Let's not get too carried away here, Don."

"Why not? I can picture it. The gravel roads around Herb's property could be the four major boulevards in town. We could name them Ocotila, Saguaro, Yucca, and Prickly Pear. The streets going North and South could benamed after Southern states and those going East and

West would be named after national parks."

"You really are getting carried away," Jamie chuckled.

"Home owners will love to have their homes built on streets with quaint names."

"Speaking of buyers and our building houses for them, how many houses to you think we should build?"

"Well, we would have 640 acres to play with. Let's say we subtract six acres for the lakes and parking areas, An acre for the club house and recreation center. Five more for green space parks. The boulevard leading to the highway should have about 10 acres set aside for commercial businesses. Of course, the roads would take up at least the equivalent of 30 acres. So, what does that up to? Fifty-two. Oh, and let's add four more for the runway, making it fifty-six. Fifty-six from 640 leaves us 584. If we build each house on a third of an acre, that means we built 438 houses."

"Don, you do realize that the Sussex Estates project only had 37 houses, don't you?"

"Yes? So? You did most of the labor on that project yourself. Here you will need a team working on all the different aspects of building a community. This could truly be your retirement project you will be administering."

Jamie remained silent. Don sat down next to him on the boulder.

"Well, dad, what are you thinking?"

"I was just thinking of you as a kid of seventeen trying to convince Cee Jay to turn his basement into an apartment. Your ideas were very convincing then and still are."

Donavon smiled. "Yeah, I remember that. That was the day I began to wonder about you and Cee Jay. I remember you and Cee Jay putting your arms around one another and singing "Those Were the Days." Robbie and

I joined you guys after our shock was gone." He paused. "You know, dad, I think that is when I fell in love with Robbie."

Jamie smiled. "Yes, those were the days. Young love blossoming." He thought for a moment. "And how is it between you guys now? Are you both still in love?"

"Dad, I'll let you in on a secret. Robbie was my first and last. I have never been with any other guy. Don't want to! And I think the same could be said for Robbie. I think God made us for one another. We're going on our fifteenth anniversary as one." Don crossed his fingers. "As we vowed: Until death do us part. I can't even imagine life without Robbie. Or him living without me. Oh, we have our spats every now and then over some silly thing but then make up for it in bed."

"That's wonderful to hear, Don. That's the way it's always been with Melissa and me. I'll share this secret with you. I've never had sex with any other female."

"What about Cee Jay?"

"Well, that's a whole other story; but I can tell you this. Since we had Robbie, I've never been with any other man. And I bet that Cee Jay hasn't either. Cee Jay and Melissa are all this bi-sexual man needs; and thank God they both accept me for who I am."

Donavon then suggested that they try to get up to the mesa, which was not part of the site they were contemplating to purchase. Don carefully maneuvered the rocks, gravel, and twist in a make believe path to the top, which rose about 80 feet above the flat field. From there they could see the entire property on one side and the barren land on the other. Jamie commented on how beautiful it was. Off in the distance he spotted a hot air balloon.

"That's probably from the Eloy air school," Don conjectured. "Robbie told me that Eloy has a world-famous jump school. Jumpers come from all over the world to train there in jumping out of air planes.

Roger has been trying to convince Robbie to make a jump with him, but I'm totally against it."

"Imagine! Jumping from an airplane. I've heard of parachuting in the military, but just for fun? That's a new one on me."

"It's a very popular sport in other countries, particularly in Germany. Roger said that most of the jumpers who come to Eloy are from Australia."

"How about that! And I never heard of it. If I were twenty-five years younger, I probably would be encouraging Cee Jay to jump with me."

"There's no age limit on jumping, Jamie. As a matter of fact, I understand that President Bush is an enthusiast."

"Hem. Let's talk about that runway over there. You indicated before that you would keep it. Why?"

"Well, for one thing, if Robbie knew there was a runway here and I suggested getting rid of it, he probably would kill me. What has Robbie been talking about incessantly?"

"I don't know. Adopting a baby or buying that damn airplane."

"That's it. He wants a Cirrus SR 22. He's been driving me crazy about buying one. He and Roger want to form a LLC to purchase and share one. If they had a runway in their backyard, they would move here in a minute. A lot of their pilot friends would also."

"Would you like to have airplanes flying off in your backyard?"

"Well, if it would make Robbie happy, I could live with it. I understand the idea of having an airpark in new communities is catching on in several parts of the country, particularly here in the Southwest.

People chip in to construct and maintain an airstrip and build their homes around it. For plane enthusiasts, it is a bit like a status symbol. Some people like to live on golf courses; land next to a golf course always increases the value of a house, even for those who don't play golf."

"Okay, we can be innovators. You, Robbie, Roger, and company could have your runway homes if it meant having you live close to us.

Now, do you think we should also have a golf course here at- what did you call it- Sonoran Desert Lakes Project?"

"Yes, of course. But let's shorten the name of our community to just 'Desert Lakes.'"

"Desert Lakes. Hem... I like it!" Jamie exclaimed. Now, where do we put this golf course?"

"Well, our airpark is on the far west of the town, so let's put the golf course on the far east side of Desert Lakes. Our man-made lake could be just north of it, perhaps having it even surrounding a few holes on the course."

"Sounds good. And I really like this spot for our new home, but it is not part of the Herb Wolf cotton property."

"All the more reason for putting a binder on the Wolf property until we can see about acquiring this land from Pinal County."

Jamie shook hands with Don on the mesa. I'm in agreement with all of your ideas, partner. Now let's go down and do some negotiating with the Wolfman."

On the way down the mesa and to Herb's house, the men briefly discussed the terms they would present.

They sat around Herb's kitchen table. All three men were drinking bottles of beer. Herb had the real estate listing as well as the description drawing of the plot. Jamie was surprised when Don started the negotiation session by asking Herb what he planned on doing with his life if he sold his property. Herb seemed surprised also and hesitated before answering.

"For one thing, I'll stop living only on my monthly Social Security checks. At this point, the sale has been so long in coming I'm not sure any more what I'd do. Maybe I'd take a trip out to California to see my daughter and her children. You know, I've never actually met my grandkids. Then I would like to visit David in Scottsdale. I've never met David's wife. So it would be nice to make peace in the family before I kick the bucket. After that I might take one of those three-week tours of Europe. I have never been outside the U.S. Not even Mexico. Never seemed to have the time."

"That sounds exciting, Herb; but I meant where would you go to live?"

"Oh, I'll probably end up in some nursing home or retirement place. There is a nice one in Casa Grande. They cook for you and have a nice dining room. They even clean your small apartment. I have some friends who live in Casa Grande and Eloy. We get together here or at their places at least once a week to play cards."

"Would you miss this house? Jamie asked.

"Sure, I would miss it. I've lived here most of my life. The wife and I raise our kids here. I have a lot of good memories here. Yeah, it would be hard for me to leave it"

"Herb, I've been thinking. How would you like our fixing this place up a bit? Building you a garage and connecting it to the house with a nice breeze-way. We would install air conditioning and a dishwasher and an over stove built-in microwave. Our company would paint the outside, refurbish the living room floor, put new carpeting in all bedroom and your office and replace the linoleum in the kitchen and bathrooms. Then you could move back in and enjoy your retirement years in the home you love."

"That sounds great, Don, but I don't have the money for those kinds of renovations."

"Jamie and I would sink $25,000 in wholesale renovations in this house, and it wouldn't cost you a penny. You would be the first resident in the community we are hoping to built here. You, see, Herb, this house is worth about $75,000 alone, and it just doesn't seem fair that we should come in here and knock this house down to make room for one we would build and get at least $150,000. We all get a win-win here. You get to stay in the house you love with a lot of fixing up and it doesn't cost you a penny. What we get is $50,000 off the price of the entire package when we reach a final price for the farm. How does that sound, Herb?"

"Well, it depends on what you are willing to pay for the farm. You know, don't you, that my asking price is $540,000?'

Jamie smiled. "My son-in-law is just trying to butter you up, Herb. Sure, your real estate agent showed us this listing in his office. I see here, however, that this listing expired three weeks ago after six months. And I suspect that this was not the first time. You know, as well as I do, that a property listed well over value is not going to sell. And there is the little fact that cotton farms are not popular in this area anymore. I bet that if the land here were listed for $500,000 you would have had offers by now. Don and I also noted that your agent wanted a 10% fee. That's reasonable and rather common for land sales, but that amounts to a whopping $50,000, leaving you with a net of $450,000.

"So, here's the deal, Herb, I am willing to pay $450,000 for the property and spend $25,000 on the house and you can own and enjoy it for the rest of your life or sell the house and make at least another $125,000"

"I'll need to have some time to think about it." Herb said.

"Even if we agreed to everything today and had a contract, you would still have three days under law to accept or reject the offer," Donavon said.

"And here's another thing for you to think of, Herb. Donavon is a lawyer so all the contracts, etc. will be written by him with no charge to you. And there will be no mortgage company interference with inspections, etc. Of course, we will need some time to check with the county on our construction project and with a hydrologist concerning water and sewer rights. We'll also need to check with the electric power company that serves the area because we want all power lines to be underground. I'm leaving for New Jersey on Friday, but Don will stay in Casa Grande or Coolidge to get the whole package wrapped up as soon as possible. I am going to give you a check for $2,000 as a good faith offer. I'll give you another $18,000 when we sign the binder. We will give you half of the balance or $215,000 in thirty days and the balance of $215,000 in six months. Don can be back here on Friday with all of this is writing." Jamie paused. "So, do we have a deal?"

"Hem. I guess so," Herb said. I will want my own lawyer to check it all out, though."

"That's understandable," Don said. "Just keep in mind that lawyers usually get big bucks and always create problems to show that they are worth their fees. Because I am a partner with Mr. Roberts, I don't get paid. Did you know, Herb, that in Arizona you do not need an attorney in a real estate deal? In New Jersey where we are from, you do."

Jamie took out his checkbook and as he was writing out the check for $2,000 told Don to write out a note saying that the $2,000 was a good faith deposit to purchase and give him, Jamie, first right of refusal If Mr. Wolf is given another offer before Friday.

As Jamie gave him the check with Don's note, Jamie noted that Herb Wolf seemed both confused and joyful at the same time.

"I certainly hope you will accept Don's generous offer for you to stay in this house after we renovate it. Don and I would love to have you as our first resident and neighbor and friend. We're big card players ourselves.

They all shook hands on the porch and said goodbye.

The next day Don convinced Jamie to go with him to a suburban community near Phoenix called Sun City. Don said that it was a successful retirement community originally built by Del Webb and that they could continue to get good ideas that they might be able to use.

On the way to Sun City, Don explained that Del Webb was a successful investor as well as a developer. "At one point Webb owned the New York Yankees," he said. "In building Sun City, Del Webb used some of the same principles of construction that Levit used back in the late 40's and 50's when he was building his Levittowns in New York and
Pennsylvania."

"And what was that?"

"Levit was a mass producer of housing. He limited the number of designs, thus being able to utilize lumber and materials in huge bulks a lot cheaper. He also was capable of building six or seven houses in the same time it took to build one conventionally."

"It sounds like assembly-line construction."

"Exactly," Don said. "Levit and Webb had construction crews for all aspects of building. Roofers, plumbers, sheetrock guys. They specialized in one thing and moved from site to site."

"Is that what you're thinking we should do in Desert Lakes?" Jamie asked.

"Well, some form of it at least. Levit was working on 4,200 acres of Long Island farmland. We only have 640 acres unless we can acquire more from Pinal County."

"Tonight, when we get back to Casa Grande, we should call Cindy's husband in Arizona City. I'd like to talk to him, share ideas with him, and if we like him, hire him to be in charge of construction."

In Sun City, the men got on a small tour bus at the Visitor Center. A volunteer acted as a tour guide. She explained to the group that Sun City was approximately seven miles long and three miles wide and had seven recreation centers and a golf course and that the tour would take them to see all of them.

Jamie was fascinated by the number, size, and condition of all these recreation centers.

"Del Web built the first rec center where the original four model homes were. A covenant was written into the deeds that all buyers had to be at least 55 years old and that every time a new owner bought a house they would have an assessment of $3000 which would go to the construction of new recreation centers. One by one the community constructed six more."

"How are they maintained," Don asked. "After all repairs and improvements are always needed on any building as it ages."

"That's a good question. Today, no resident lives more than a mile from any rec center. The centers are hubs for the recreational, social, and cultural lives of our residents. If you join a rec center you pay an annual fee of $500 which entitles you to use the facilities at all of them. The centers are run by a few paid employees and many volunteers. Sun City is know as "The City of Volunteers" and we are very proud of them. I myself am a volunteer. We have an elected Board overseeing the Home Owners Association which controls all operations. At last count, I think we had 110 clubs in town, ranging from pottery to railroading and orchestral, dramatics, dance, etc. No matter what your interest are, we have a club to satisfy that interest. Considering that most health clubs in the area charge $500 for a membership, just about all residence are happy to pay the $500 rec center fee."

"Does that include golf courses?" Jamie asked.

"No. Miniature golf is free at all centers, but to play on the courses, there is a greens fee."

Jamie leaned into Donavon and whispered. "I really like the idea of charging $3,000 for a real estate transaction and $500 yearly for maintenance of the rec centers. A HOA will take the burden off the developer and keep the amenities up to date."

Another tourist on the jitney asked about the residents.

"At first most of the home buyers were from Phoenix and the surrounding area. But then we started advertising out of state, particularly in places with a colder climate like Wisconsin and Minnesota. Retirees want to get away from shoveling snow. A good third of our residents are snowbirds, meaning they come here in the winter and return to their native state in the summer. At the Mountain View rec center, they started putting a flag from each state in the auditorium. Today, all fifty states are recognized."

Don leaned in to whisper to Jamie. "Do you know the papers for Oshkosh and Boise?"

Jamie smiled. "No, but we soon will be advertising in them."

When the tour ended back at the Bell Center Recreation Center, Jamie and Don thanked their guide. Both men found it interesting.

"I'm glad you suggested coming here, Don," Jamie said. "By learning how other developers built their communities we are better to select the good and bad of each. Let's get back to Casa Grande now and start planning Desert Lakes."

Jamie ended his "story."

"So, there you have it, folks. That's how Desert Lakes was begun. I must give Don credit for most of it. I could go on telling you all about design, construction crews, marketing, bulk purchasing of appliances, etc. but maybe you know all that stuff already or can get it from Don when he gets better. I'll tell you this, though, for those first two years I never worked so long and hard as I did. But I enjoyed every minute of it. As you know, until last weeks' tragedy, Desert Lakes was a great cultural and financial success.

"By the way, while I was talking, I saw Robbie get up and quietly leave the room."

"Yes, dad. I think he was crying. I think you hit a raw nerve when you mentioned that bit about him and Don adopting a baby," Barbie said. "I'll try talking to him."

Chapter 7

✦✦✦✦✦

Roger found Robbie sitting on one of the swings on the patio between the main house and the casita. Jamie said the swings were for his grandchildren, but he and Melissa enjoyed it themselves as much as watching the kids at play. Robbie and Donavon often "thought things out together" while gently swinging up and down and side by side. When Robbie left the family room during Jamie's talk about the founding of Desert Lakes, Roger knew Robbie was upset and he also knew where Robbie was going.

"Hey, buddy. Isn't it a bit cold to be out here with just a sweater on?" Roger sat on the swing next to Robbie.

"No. I'm used to this Arizona climate." He paused briefly. "This is a very warm alpaca sweater." He hugged himself and ran his hands over the sleeves. "Don gave me this sweater last Christmas." Both men remained silent for a moment.

"Robbie, your dad volunteered to drive me over to my house to get my car. You shouldn't drive me to Tucson tonight. I'll park in the lot down at TUS. We think that you should stay here with the kids and your family. Barbie said that she would like to go to the hospital with you. She's hoping that she can at least get to see Don tonight."

Robbie smiled. He patted Roger's leg. "Thanks, Roger." He paused. "Did you know that Barbie had a big crush on Don in their senior year at Mountain Ridge? It took her a long time for her to realize that I did too. It took her even longer to realize that Don had a bigger crush on me than on her."

"Well, she got a good man in Greg."

"And has given Don and me a wonderful niece and nephew. Don loves those kids as if they were his own."

Both men were silent again.

"Well, it's time for me to be heading out, Captain. I'll see you in a couple of days."

"Thanks, Roger. I'll call you, if there is any news." As Roger started walking back into the house, Robbie called to him, "You're a good friend, Roger."

Roger turned to him. "So are you, Robbie. The best! Always have been." Both simultaneously saluted.

Robbie kick-started his swing into action as a tear trickled down his cheek.

A few minutes later, Barbie came out of the house. She was wrapped in a heavy coat. She handed her brother a serape. "Here, mom said you should put this around you." She sat on the swing. "I thought it was supposed to be warm here in Arizona. It's damn cold here."

"Night's get pretty cold in the Sonoran Desert, sis, but you will get acclimated."

"Not me. I'd prefer to see snow on the trees. I was just talking to Greg and he said Doylestown was having a heavy snowfall. They are predicting a foot before it's over."

They both remained deep in thought as they swung up and down.

When they stopped and sat next to one another, Barbie said, "I think dad hit a nerve with you when he said that you and Don were considering adopting."

"Yeah, kind of."

"I didn't know that you guys were thinking of having a family."

"We didn't discuss it with our families. But that was five years ago. Don was the one who first brought up the subject. At first, I liked the idea, but then decided against it. I didn't think we were ready. We were too busy. Don was opening his office in Doylestown and studying for the Pennsylvania bar and I was still working on my certifications and flying charters. Our own careers were too time-consuming. We had trouble adjusting to our own lives let alone caring for a baby."

He stopped. "I also wasn't that keen on adoption. Oh, I wanted to have a family but somehow having a child that was parented by others just didn't seem right."

"What do you mean?"

"You know, inherited characteristics. When you and Greg had your babies, you knew what you were getting. Some kids take after their mothers, some take after their fathers."

"I know just what you mean, Robbie. Both Missy and Greg Junior are more like their father than me."

"But at least you knew who their father was. And you wanted to increase the love you had for one another. I wanted my child to be an extension of myself or Don. I thought long and hard about inheriting not only looks and mannerisms, but also intelligence and good and bad health issues that parents may be passing on to their children. Sure, all babies are beautiful and cute, but as they start maturing, what's in their genes begins to emerge. I read an article that said that children of alcoholics and drug users are more likely to become addicts themselves.

Granted, Don is more intelligent than me but I'm pretty smart too. I did graduate from Rutgers and am a certified pilot. I feared that if we adopted a child, he or she might not have similar mental abilities. When a husband and wife naturally have a child, they love and totally accept what God gives them. I guess I am just not altruistic enough to be that accepting."

"I understand what you are saying, Robbie. But let's face it, Robbie, gay guys just can't have kids in the 'natural' way God intends."

"Perhaps I'm too selfish. Don showed me a study that said that there are 40,000 gay couples in the United States who are raising children, biological or adopted. But adoption is not for me."

"So why did you get upset and leave the room when dad mentioned it?"

"Because since Donavon told dad we were considering adoption, things have changed."

"How?"

"It's a long story, Barbie, but I'll try telling you in a shortened way." He paused briefly in order to collect his thoughts. "Do you remember the girl that Don hired as his paralegal when he opened the Doylestown office?"

"Yes, I remember Jessica. She was a very pretty young gal. Intelligent. Friendly. Greg and I actually had her over at our house for dinner a few times. I remember that she was at our place once with you and Don. She was a fun person, and she once helped Greg with some legal questions he had at the college. Whatever happened to her?"

"Don came out to her before he hired her, and the three of us became friends. Don thought the world of her; and when he opened his office in Coolidge, he convinced her to move here to Arizona. He gave her a big enough incentive bonus for her to put a down payment on her own house here in Desert Lakes."

"I think I can guess where this story is going," Barbie said, "but go on."

"Last New Year's Eve, Don and I hosted a small party for some friends and colleagues. Don, of course, invited Jessica. A few months before, I met a stewardess by the name of Maria. Maria was one of the funniest girls I ever met. You know the type. You can't help loving her charms and wit. She was attractive as well as witty. She knew how to put down aggressive pilots and passengers without hurting their feelings. Maria and I spent a lot of time together whenever we met or at a lay-over on the same flight. I never told her that I was gay or married to another guy; but I did invite her to our party. I thought that she and Roger should meet and that they would make a nice couple."

"Roger? Robbie, when are you going to stop playing cupid to him?"

"Well, it turned out that Jessica and Maria hit it off immediately and became good friends, and then lovers. They were married in June and Maria moved in with Jessica here in Desert Lakes."

"Hem. Seems like Desert Lakes is becoming a New Hope West."

"Don't be such a smart ass, Barbie."

"So, what is it about Jessica and her partner Maria you want to tell me?"

"A few months ago, the four of us were having dinner and the girls told us that they wanted to start a family themselves. They both wanted to have a baby but couldn't decide which one should have it because they both want to experience pregnancy and raise both babies together. They went to an adoption agency and even went to a sperm bank in Phoenix, but Jessica was against that for pretty much the same reasons I was. Jessica was against the idea of a total stranger getting paid by a sperm bank for jerking off in a vial. Maria joked with Don, asking me if I would free Don for an evening.

"Hem. That sounds pretty gross."

"We thought so, also. But later Don and I discussed it privately. We thought that surrogate parenting might be a win-win for the girls as well as ourselves. We know these women well, and they know us. In a way,

Maria's flagrant remark could be taken as a compliment. She was telling us that she wanted the true father of her child to be like Don or me." "So?"

"So, we discussed it again with Jessica and Maria, and they loved the idea. Surrogacy is an option for gay men and lesbians who want to be biologically connected to their children. In the LGBT community surrogacy pregnancy is most commonly achieved using an egg donor, gestational carrier, and in vitro fertilization. Same-sex couples have to first decide who will be genetically related to the child. We had to decide whose sperm and whose egg would be used.

Since Don and I both wanted to be fathers and both Jessica and Maria wanted to be mothers, Don and I wanted to use both of our sperms mixed to fertilize both women. None of us would in effect know from whom the winning little swimmer would be to fertilize each woman's egg."

"Wow! Talk about 'planned parentage'! This beats everything I ever heard of.

"It would give all of us the opportunity to fulfill our dream of having our own family while maintaining a genetic link to our children. And living close to one another, the kids could get to know and grow up together…be playmates. Share things, as most siblings in any family do."

"Very interesting," Barbie explained. "But which baby do you get and which one do the women get as their own to raise?"

"That's an important issue that we really haven't decided yet. I think Don would prefer to keep the boy. I don't care if our baby is a boy or girl. And Jessica, I think, would prefer to raise a girl, while Maria is like me; she doesn't care."

"What if both children are boys or girls? Or if one of the women has twins?

"Those questions, we haven't put into writing yet," Robbie said,

"because we have two questions to resolve first." "And what are they?" Barbie asked.

"First, we live in Arizona. Surrogacy contracts are illegal in Arizona and, therefore, cannot be created or enforced in a court of law. Donavon is an attorney here and says that he can write up what he called a "memorandum of understanding." Ours is not a traditional surrogacy so both he and Jessica will be extra careful in preparing it. Don said that he would also like another practicing lawyer who may be more familiar with

Arizona surrogacy to check it."

He remained silent for several minutes.

"And the second question which needs to be resolved? You said before that there were two issues," Barbie said.

"Will Don be alive to become a father?' Robbie softly said. Both remained silent and moved about on their swings.

"Mom and Dad don't know about all of this yet, do they."

"No, and I don't want them to until it's all settled one way or the other."

"Right. Thank you, little brother, for sharing it with me. Now, let's go inside for a bite to eat before going to the hospital. I expect Don is going to jump out of his hospital bed and give me a big hug as soon as he sees me tonight." Barbie grabbed her brother's hand and led him back into the house.

Reentering his parents' home, Robbie was overcome with anguish.

He wanted to get away from everyone. He wanted to be alone with his thoughts of Don. He wanted Don so much. Without him, nothing seemed to matter. Did these people know? Could they understand his anguish? Robbie felt that his own life, the life that he had since he met Don was now taken from him. All the joy of being alive! How could Don be anything, but the way he had been? Robbie knew he was beginning a new life; he was being forced into adulthood where there was suffering and death. Nothing would be the same after this.

He felt their eyes on him. Worried. Silent. Who could talk? The kids in the corner having fun coloring in a book. The senseless joy of childhood. The mother, pretending the fuss over preparing a casserole was important. The father, playing with a remote device that kept changing the vision of his world, not wanting to face the one he was presently living. His old teacher, sitting, silent, miles away in thoughts that once were real. His sister trying to console him. Not realizing that they would all be dead themselves within a blink of God's eye. Why should he pretend to eat? He had heard of death. Loved ones, gone. The boy he was never felt death. Now he did. Now, he, too, was near death.

Cee Jay once spoke of Sisyphus. ... Don....Robbie.... Together, they had pushed that boulder up the mountain. Why couldn't they have more… More, what? ... Time to be together. To grow old together Now…starting all over.

Pushing that rock up the mountain by himself. Why? …. To have some other sick human being end it for some stupid, meaningless pimple on the ass of progress. Could mankind ever progress? … All eyes on him.

A mother's touch. "I know how you feel, Robbie. But you must have something to eat before you go to the hospital tonight. It's lasagna. I made it just the way you and Don used to love it when you were teenagers."

All Robbie wanted was to get to the hospital as quickly as possible.

Chapter 8

When Robbie and Barbie arrived at the hospital, the ward nurse gave them some very good news.

"Mr. Rice is off the ventilator and is conscious. He is still under sedation, however; but should be able to recognize you. He will be able to say a few words, but you should not expect him to do much talking tonight." She smiled. "So, you do most of the talking, okay."

"For my sister, that should be easy. She never shuts up." Robbie said with a big grin.

"Well, I'm glad that Mr. Rice is now able to have more visitors. If he falls asleep, that means you should leave. Okay?"

Barbie jabbed her brother's shoulder. "See, I told you he'd jump up and give me a big hug tonight."

"Well, you should not count on that tonight. His arm is still in a cast and he must remain in bed."

As they approached Don's room, for the first time in days, Robbie felt that he was walking on clouds. His friend, his lover, his alter ego, his husband was going to live!

Don's eyes were closed and he appeared to be asleep; but when Robbie kissed his forehead, he opened his eyes and blinked. He smiled and mumbled Robbie's name.

"Look who I brought to see you today," Robbie said.

Once again, Don blinked he in an effort to focus. "Barbie," he said in a whisper, "What brings you here?"

Barbie bent to pat his brow. "I've come to see how my best senior prom date ever is doing. I heard that you were playing cowboys and Indians out here in Arizona."

For the first time in what seemed like an eternity, Robbie saw a smile on Don's face.

"I guess... I'm still alive," he softly spoke with difficulty. He attempted to sit up, and Barbie immediately adjusted his pillow while Robbie helped him sit up.

"I blacked out at the meeting." He stopped. "Shooting," he mumbled. "Where am I?"

"You're in Casa Grande Medical Center," Robbie said. "You have been unconscious for four days."

"But I know you were here a few times. I was aware...." He started coughing.

"Yes, I was here, love. I came back from Jamacia as soon as I could."

"You do remember the shooting at the HOA meeting?" Barbie asked.

"Yes." Don lifted his left hand to his throat, indicating that he found it difficult to speak; but he managed to ask, "Randy?"

"He's dead."

Don closed his eyes and shook his head, "And Maxwell?"

"You killed him."

"Oh, my God," Don managed.

"For a guy who never used a gun before, you proved to have a better aim than Maxwell; but he managed to seriously injure you in the arm and you lost a lot of blood. There were other complications as well."

Donavon touched the cast with his left hand. "This?" is all he could say.

"We don't know about that yet. We do know that the bullet ruptured an artery and fractured a part of your elbow. The bullet had to be surgically removed."

There was a long pause before Don spoke again. "Barbie, how are the kids? Are they here in Arizona?"

"Yes, and they want you to go home as soon as possible. They don't like staying at Mom and Dad's casita. They said they want to stay with you and Uncle Robbie. You guys give them candy and play with them."

Don smiled and paused. "Do Jessica and Marie know about all this?"

"Yes, and they have been praying for your complete recovery. Our 'mommies' are as anxious as their 'daddies.'"

"Tell Jessica to write up a draft of the 'Memorandum'. I'll get to it as soon as possible.

"Robbie are you still sure you want this? You may have to care for me as well as our baby."

"More than ever," Robbie said kissing his husband's hand.

"Good. Me too."

"Robbie told me about what you guys are planning, and I'm ecstatic for you," Barbie said. "You two will make wonderful parents."

Don smiled and raised and lowered his head. After a moment, he said, "How's Cee Jay?"

"Like all of us, he has been crying and praying for you. He was here with Mom and Dad when they brought you to the hospital that horrible night. Now that you can have visitors, I'm sure he will want to be here. The three of them will be here tomorrow morning and Barbie and I will be here in the evening. Okay?"

The two men held one another's hand firmly.

Barbie was the first to speak again. "Perhaps tomorrow you will be able to tell us what caused this big shoot-out at the O.K. Corral."

After a moment, Donavon said, "Robbie, in my file cabinet at home, you'll find a file on Maxwell. Give the file to Cee Jay and have him and your dad bring it here tomorrow. Barbie, maybe you will like to come with them in the morning to learn all the details of what led to the shooting. Robbie, come with Mom tomorrow evening." He started coughing again.

A nurse entered the room with a small pitcher of water and a plastic cup. "Looks like you need another pill, Mr. Rice. So, say goodbye to your visitors." She turned to Robbie. "He really needs to rest now. He'll be fine in the morning."

On the way out of the ward, Robbie whispered to his sister, "Big Nurse Ratched in there is really a dike bitch."

"What? Oh, yeah." It sank in and Barbie chuckled. "You really are sick, little brother."

Chapter 9

◆ ◆ ◆ ◆ ◆

As Jamie, Cee Jay, and Barbie walked down the hall to Don's room, they knew Don was well on his way to recovery. They heard his usual optimistic and strong voice speaking on the telephone. "That's great, Robbie. Tell Jessica by this time next month she'll be pregnant. Yep, I'll be up to it." He paused for Robbie's question. "That's not really up to me, but I'll be ready for anything except shooting hoops with you for a while." He paused for a moment to look up and smile. "Hey, Dad, Barbie, and Cee Jay just came in, so I got to go." He paused. "Yes, I love you, too. I'll see you and Mom tonight."

All four shared their exuberance. Jamie and Cee Jay took turns kissing Donavon on the cheek, and Barbie kissed his forehead. She remarked how more awake and handsome he seemed than last night. Jamie wanted to know if he had any idea when he would be able to leave the hospital.

Cee Jay handed him the file that Robbie gave to him earlier. "I just scanned through it on the way here," Cee Jay said. "It's interesting. I was surprised by how thorough your notes on Maxwell are. I guess that's the lawyer in you to keep track of things. You may need this file, if the prosecutor calls for an inquest."

"Thanks, Dad. I thought you might help out with that. Barbie wanted to know everything about the shooting, so I could review this material with you as I bring her up to date."

Jamie interrupted. "By the way, Don, there is a guy out in the waiting room who wants to interview you from the *Tucson Star*. He was here the night of the shooting also. His name's Guy Neville. Here's his card."

"Oh, sure, I know Guy. He's a good reporter." He turned to ask Barbie to invite him into the room. "I guess you all should be in on the story." When Barbie left the room, Don explained to the men that he first met

Guy when they played football as red shirts at Rutgers. Don renewed his friendship with him when he read an article that he wrote in the Tucson paper. "We lost contact after college and I was surprised to learn that he was now on the staff of ***The Star.***"

As soon as Barbie and Guy entered the room, Guy went to Don and shook his free hand.

"I bet I know why you are here, Guy," Don said, "but it's good to see you, buddy."

"Actually, I'm here for three reasons," Guy Neville said. "The first is to see how you are. You gave all of us a pretty good scare the other night." "My doctor seems to think I'll live a bit longer," Don joked.

"Good to hear that. Now, for the professional reason I'm here: Are you going to run for the House?"

"Well, I still want to, but the answer is not really up to me, is it? I don't know if the Democratic party will support me. If they do, I'm in, but if not, I go back to being a country lawyer. And that's okay with me."

"Why wouldn't you be their candidate, Don? I think you're perfect for the job."

"Thanks for your confidence in me, Guy. Now if we can get your paper and the Party on board, that would be good."

"So, what's the problem?"

"Well, for starters, Pinal County already has a gay sheriff. Can they still handle a gay representative? And a gay representative who is also a married gay man with a family by next November."

Almost in unison, all three men exclaimed: "What?"

"Yes, Robbie and I have decided to start a family." He smiled broadly. "Frankly, that's more important to me than being a Representative."

Cee Jay was the first to respond. "That's wonderful news, Don!" Turning to Jamie, he said, "Imagine us being surrogate grandfathers, Jamie."

"Well, I already am a grandfather, but I am happy for you Don.....if you think Robbie is up to the job of being a father." He paused. "I guess you guys will now be the poster boys of the LGBT community."

"That's really great news, Don," the reporter exclaimed. "Is it okay for me to write about it?"

"Nothing other than the fact that my husband and I very much want to have a baby ASAP is okay. Anything else about it at this time, will have to wait to see what happens. Okay?"

"Of course, Don. I understand."

"The other thing that must be considered is that I've made it very clear that I will fight very hard in Washington for changes in gun control. I don't know how the electorate will accept that now, knowing that I shot and killed a man with my own gun."

"But that was in self-defense," Barbie offered.

"Yeah, but I can picture how the GOP will spin it," Don said.

As if deliberately changing the subject, the reporter said that he had another reason for visiting Don. He told him that he wanted his advice on writing a book for which he was currently doing research.

"Don, I know that you would like some drastic changes made to the Second Amendment as well as directing greater government funding toward mental health. That's all well and good, but I'm exploring another avenue. Is early detection of potential killers even possible? By diverting monies toward mental health, are we just setting up new, expensive agencies that are so regulated by privacy issues that the potential killer cannot be detected in time to avert his deeds? For the most part, I believe that we may be continuing to ignore or minimize the symptoms of a killer until it's too late. I am exploring other ways that we may use to reduce senseless shootings and suicides."

"Wow! What a great subject! I'm not sure I can help you, however. Sociologists and psychologists as well as criminal detectives have been on the issue of what makes a murderer for a long time. There are those that say some killers may be influenced by early childhood environmental factors and some who go so far as believing that some humans are just born with atavistic genes that may lead them to crime and murder. Many murders and suicides are related to the military where men and women are taught to kill, and hatred toward a common enemy is so instilled deep in a person's psyche that the human life of anyone who opposes our personal views is an enemy and not worth living. The Existentialist might say that a murderer makes a good combat soldier and vice versa."

Guy Neville blurted, "Precisely!"

Don continued. "No doubt childhood experiences and environment may have influencing factors as well. A child who has been abused may grow up to be an abuser and ultimately a killer." He turned toward Cee Jay. "Cee Jay, you used to say that society never stops paying for poor education. Perhaps we may apply that same maxim to killers. Society breeds killers among poor, impoverished citizens who struggle to rise above it the same way an animal might kill to survive. So, Guy, it may boil down to simple economics. Improve the standard of living and you may be bringing down the number of killings."

"As always, you have expressed some interesting views. Thanks, Don. Now, what are your perceptions on the Desert Lakes murderer?"

"My sister-in-law Barbara Otenburg here wanted to know the same thing. I must admit that I don't know precisely what the catalyst that caused Robert Maxwell to kill Randal Scott and me as well as potentially others at that meeting. I can tell you, however, that I thought it might happen because I kept a bit of a journal or file on Mr. Maxwell. After a while, I believed it was predictable, and that is why I bought a gun and took lessons on how to use and aim it without telling anyone." "Why didn't you tell me?" Jamie asked.

"Because I didn't want to scare you and others and possibly even cause more harm. I simply wanted to defend myself and others who might be victimized by Maxwell, whom I deduced was a madman before the meeting. Unfortunately, I saw that he shot Randy and as soon as he aimed his revolver at me, I shot him as he was shooting at me. I am sorry that in the mayhem, Randy was killed, and I killed Maxwell. Thank God that his aim didn't end my life, but it did enough to seriously injure me. The doctor told me this morning that I will be able to use my arm again after some physical therapy. He told me I will always have some stiffness in lifting my arm." He chuckled. "I guess Robbie will be playing basketball with Roger a lot more than me from now on."

"Do you mind sharing your file notes with me?" Guy asked.

"No, not at all. Barbie wanted to know more about the shooting also. That's why Cee Jay brought the file this morning. If you have the time now, stay a while and hear the whole story of how Desert Lakes became a murder scene."

"Sure, I'll be glad to stay and hear what you have to say. If you folks don't mind my being here, that is." Guy Neville looked around the room to the other visitors who were all seating around the hospital bed. Jamie, Cee Jay, and Barbie all nodded in agreement.

Barbie was the first to speak. "So, when did you first begin to think of Robert Maxwell as a killer?"

"Long before I thought of him as a potential killer, I thought of him as somewhat odd. You might say 'different.' I got that impression the first time I met him. That was before he and his wife Mary even moved to Desert Lakes."

"Really?" Cee Jay asked.

"As you know, I always met with prospective buyers. After they had the tour and sat with our sales manager for a while, they would send buyers to me for the contract signing.

"That's when I first met Robert and Mary Maxwell."

"Yes. But what was different about Maxwell that caused you to redflag him?" Jamie asked.

"Two things, actually. First, his appearance. He came into my office wearing baggy jeans. Most men who bought houses came in to sign a sales contract were fairly well dressed. He was not; his wife was well dressed but casually. He obviously had not shaved in several days; he didn't have a beard or a five o'clock; he had whiskers. He always had whiskers. Even at that last board meeting, he had whiskers. It was as though he never shaved. He just trimmed his whiskers. He wore wireframed, round glasses. His piercing green-gray eyes, would glare behind those tinted glasses, and with his whiskers, he seemed … What shall I say… different?"

"Also," Don continued, "I noticed that he did all the talking. Most husbands are only interested in the financial aspects of a sales contract, but not him. He questioned and chose everything. From the color of the kitchen appliances and countertops, to landscaping, from light fixtures to the color of the front door, from the type of tile to the color of the bedroom carpet, he did the selecting, while Mary just sat there smiling and occasionally nodding in agreement with her husband.

"Jessica, my paralegal, also had noticed an abnormality in his mortgage application. She drew it to my attention that he had listed his employment as the owner of a tool manufacturing plant that he sold for $450,000 in Washington state. He also sold his home in Washington and cleared $210,000 on it. He did not show any bank accounts, but Mary had $150,000 in savings which she got in a divorce settlement from her previous husband. They had $810,000 in the bank and were applying for a mortgage on a house that, with all their options, cost $158,000 and after the 20% down, the mortgage was for $126,400."

"Seems to me the Maxwells were planning to retire on their savings," Jamie offered. "They probably felt it was better to pay a mortgage on the house here and to use it to get credit than take it from their savings."

"You're probably right about that, Dad. But here's the really strange part: Their application for the mortgage was turned down. They ended up paying cash for the house."

"Hem. Another red flag!" Jamie said.

"Right. But I didn't question them about it, and the deal was closed. Both Jessica and I were interested in knowing why they were turned down, so Jessica did a bit of searching for answers on her own. We discovered some pretty interesting facts about Maxwell. First, he did not sell his company for $450,000. Jessica called the company and spoke to the real owner. Turns out, Maxwell never "owned" the company. He was made a supervisor when he made a $4,000 profit-sharing stock deal. As a supervisor, he became obsessive and was always criticizing the work of other employees. Some even quit rather than put up with him. The real owner said that when the employees really began to complain, he realized that Maxwell felt that no one could do anything better than he. Maxwell simply refused to delegate work projects and criticized the work of others. Eventually, he had to fire him. He was given a farewell bonus of $4500 or $500 in severance and a return of his $4,000 in stock."

"That would certainly explain some of his actions here at Desert Lakes," Cee Jay said.

"Indeed, it would," Don said. "And it also explains why the Bank of America rejected his mortgage application. Another interesting fact that Jessica uncovered was that Mary and Robert were married for less than a year. Mary was wife number three for Maxwell. He and the first wife were married for only two years. There are court records that the second wife charged him for physical and mental abuse before divorcing him. That marriage also ended after a few years. None of the marriages produced children."

"That's amazing!" Jamie exclaimed. "How did Jessica uncover all of those things?"

"Well, if you know the right people to contact, it's surprisingly easy. And with the help of your computer, you can learn just about everything about anybody today."

A pert candy striper entered the room with a tray. "Lunchtime, Mr. Rice," she called out.

"Our master chef prepared this delicious gourmet lunch just for your first meal in Chateau Casa Grande." She placed the tray on the bed table. "Do you think you can handle it alone with your left hand? If not, perhaps one of these fine people can assist you."

She turned to the guests in the room. "If you folks don't mind cafeteria food, we have a dining room downstairs next to the gift shop, but Mr. Rice really should relax while quietly enjoying his hamburger feast. Perhaps, if our patient is up to it, you can come back in an hour or so."

"Oh, I am sure that I'll be up to it," Don said.

"Good, because I want to hear the rest of this story," Barbie said.

"Let's go to that fine dining facility downstairs and give Don some time to rest and wash up. I'm treating today," Jamie said.

Guy Neville padded Don's shoulder. "I'll be back in an hour or so." The others all agreed.

Chapter 10

——— ✦✦✦✦✦ ———

After lunch, the guests went into the gift shop. Their presents for Donavon included four get-well balloons that Jamie and Barbie bought after some discussion about what color they should be. Jamie wanted all the colors of the Pride Rainbow, while Barbie wanted the colors of Mountain Ridge High, so they finally settled with two blues, one yellow, and one red. Cee Jay bought a bouquet of red and yellow roses and Guy selected a kid-sized soft football saying that his gift was best because "it would give Don something to squeeze with his good hand." Cee Jay and Jamie thought that was hilarious, while Barbie smirked and said, "You two are sick."

Entering Don's room, Jamie insisted on relating Guy's remark, which Don also thought was funny, and thanked Guy for the football, but added, "I hope I will be able to squeeze something else soon." Don also gushed over the beautiful flowers that Cee Jay gave him.

"Don, over lunch Cee Jay told us that he never saw Mary and Maxwell together. She seemed to always be by herself at the clubhouse, pool, or other activities."

"I would agree with that, but a lot of women did things by themselves or with female friends. Husbands usually did things together also like playing cards, hanging out at the bar, or playing golf. But Cee Jay's right. Maxwell never did anything with his wife. Even at social events, she would go off with a group of ladies while he just sat and listened to whatever group of men he was around. If anyone went to him to open a conversation, he would respond politely and then curtly be dismissive. I would observe him often lurking around on his own at night. He was, indeed, pretty much a loner."

"Mr. Roberts said that at one time he was a member of the HOA board," Guy Neville said. "How did that happen. Usually, Board members are gregarious. Aren't they?"

Don smiled. "Yeah, small-town politician types. From the time he moved to Desert Lakes he was at every Board meeting. Our monthly meetings average about thirty to forty people, but that usually includes husbands and wives. Maxwell usually just sat by himself, however, and never really participated, but after the first year, he started asking questions, questioning Board decisions, and complaining about this or that. After a while, he became a nuisance and got a bit of a reputation for being vocally negative about everything." "Such as?" Guy Neville asked.

"I started keeping a file on him when at one meeting he demanded that the Board revise the by-laws to include what colors homeowners could paint their front doors. He claimed that one owner on Calle Ocotillo actually repainted the front door yellow. He claimed that the owner should have asked the Board's permission before painting it ....

and these were his exact words....'that ugly Puerto Rican yellow.'" "Wow! The man wasn't too prejudiced, was he" Barbie said.

"I remember that," Cee Jay offered. "But what surprised me was that no one seemed to object to his remark."

"Yes, silence is a form of agreement," Don said. "But Randy, who was the vice president at that time, did, I think, defuse the situation by quickly thanking him for his idea and that the Board would take the issue of revising the by-laws up in an executive meeting in the future." "So, did the Board do anything?" Neville asked.

"We did have an executive meeting the following week, but we mostly talked about how inappropriate his reference to Puerto Ricans was. I congratulated Randy for the way he handled this situation; but advised that we should not get involved in the issue of changing the bylaws for one resident's objection to the color yellow.

"Surprisingly, Maxwell was still on the issue at the next monthly meeting. The agenda for our open monthly meetings permitted residents to ask questions and to voice suggestions, etc. after our business and any special reports were made. Maxwell wanted to know if we had met and had given any thought to the painting of one's front door without the permission of the Board. Bill O'Reilly, who was president at the time, told him that the Board felt that they did not want to jeopardize an owner's right to paint his doors any color he chose. Then Maxwell rebutted him by saying that he thought the current board was not interested in keeping the value of homes in Desert Lakes up. Bill then told him that if he didn't like the way this Board acted, Maxwell should run for the Board himself at the next Annual Meeting. Maxwell mumbled that that is what he intended to do. I made a specific note of this because it reminded me of his former employer's statement that everything had to be done his way, or not at all. This was, I believed then and still do, the worst aspect of his psychological personality.

"After that Maxwell did make a suggestion which the Board and the community liked.

Because we did not have our own police force and it was not always convenient to call for the sheriff's office, Maxwell asked if he could organize a Neighborhood Watch program. He really did do a good job of holding several meetings to explain what a Neighborhood Watch would offer Desert Lakes. He brought in the Sheriff to speak to us about it and also the leader of the group in Arizona City. He gathered petitions and called for volunteers."

"Well, how did that work out?" Barbie asked.

"Most people liked the idea," Don continued. "The problem is that most residents here are retirees who want the Watch but are not willing to volunteer to do the work. Younger people, like myself and Robbie and Roger just don't have the time to devote to it. In addition to keeping watch for unusual behaviors and strangers during the day, Maxwell wanted people to sign up for what he called 'night beats.' Even getting volunteers to distribute signs for people to put in their windows was difficult and many residents thought signs alone were ineffective; people said they preferred to have security devices in their homes instead. To date, thank God here in Desert Lakes, we have had a few incidents of husband-wife disputes, but no major crimes. Robbie and I did see Maxwell walking around at all hours of the night a few times, but I think that after a while, the whole idea faded. One result of the Neighborhood Watch idea, however, was that Maxwell's name got recognized in the community.

Shortly after the Neighborhood Watch thing seemed over, Maxwell made another complaint at a Board meeting. As part of all purchase contracts, Roberts Development was to plant one live citrus tree or cactus plant of the buyer's choice as well as provide gravel for the front yard. Additional gravel for back and side yards was an option at a low cost. Most buyers did select this option and many residents did also opt for additional plantings."

"That sounds like a generous offer by Dad," Barbie said. "The option for additional landscaping was also good. So, what was Maxwell's complaint?"

"Well, some people went a little too far with landscaping their yards for Robert Maxwell. Many owners whose homes abutted the golf course wanted grass in their backyards rather than gravel and paid for professional gardeners from Casa Grande and Eloy to come in and plant grass and take care of it. Eventually, a few snowbirds throughout the community wanted their Arizona property to remind them of their homes up north with grass and more greenery, etc. Some actually removed the gravel around the front and replaced it with grass.

"Maxwell had two arguments against this. The first one kind of did make sense. He complained about the water that was necessary to maintain lawns, particularly in the burning sun of Arizona. He felt watering was a waste of a natural element that should be conserved. He also complained of the noise factor when lawns had to be mowed. Both are real concerns, but his second reason was really off the wall. He claimed that homes with trees, plants, and grass reduced the value of homes where owners could not afford the upkeep. Again, he argued for a change in HOA bylaws that would not permit any grass and succulent plantings."

"That one must have gone over very well," Barbie snickered.

Jamie entered the conversation. "Actually, it did disturb a lot of folks here. Maxwell got another loudmouth to join his cause for conservation. The conservationists never talked about the fact that all homes have individual meters and owners pay for their own water usage." "So, what became of that argument?" Barbie asked.

"The board did send out a letter to all homeowners saying that we live in the desert and should be more conservative with water. The letter suggested planting cactus and other things that use less water. The board did not change the by-laws and I guess the letter was sufficient, because we never heard about it again," Jamie said.

"Was there any reason to believe that there may have been a personal grudge between Maxwell and you, Don?" the reporter asked.

"Oh, yeah. Big time!" Don exclaimed. "Maxwell called me one night and invited me to go out with him for a dinner at a restaurant in Eloy. He said that he wanted to discuss something with me personally before taking it to the board. I was hesitant but curious, so I did agree to the date.

At first, he was very pleasant as we spoke about how much better the climate was in Arizona than where we had come from; he was from the Northwest and I from New Jersey. Then we talked about the excellent wines the restaurant specialized in. He seemed to try to impress me as a wine connoisseur, and I pretended to be interested. But eventually, he began to turn the conversation around. He bluntly said that he was curious as to why I was on the board when the covenants clearly said that Roberts Development, of which I was a partner, would turn the daily operations of Desert Lakes to an independently elected HOA after two years or when the population reached two hundred households.

"I tried being calm as I explained to him that I was not a member of the board. That I did not hold any elected or appointed position on the board. I did, however, assist in the organization of the first HOA board. I had agreed to give legal advice to the board as a whole on a purely *pro bono* basis until such time as the board would vote to retain its own attorney whom they would pay at the going rate. I told him that I don't attend any regular meetings unless asked to by the board. Then he asked me if I didn't consider that being a conflict of interest. I had to bite my tongue before I answered that question to tell him that questions that may be reflective of my personal interests had never come up and, if they did, I would tell the board I was to be recused. The board was happy to get my free legal advice on several issues.

"Then he asked if I was aware that a second Black man had moved into Desert Lakes. I told him that I did, that I met with all new residents purchasing homes here. When he asked why I permitted another 'Blackie' to buy into Desert Lakes, I felt like spitting on the bastard; but told him that as long as anyone wanted to live here and could afford to, he had every right to live here or anywhere else he wanted. That, I told, him was his constitutional right under the Civil Rights and Housing Acts Then his face shrugged and he gestured with his hand as if to say "So what?"

"Then he really pissed me off," Don continued. "He said that I could have made up some kind of an excuse or found something that would have kept him from buying. You could have told him something to the effect that he wouldn't like it here because there weren't enough of his kind for him to socialize with.

"That's when I nearly walked out of the restaurant, but the food was good and I thought this idiot should be taught something about American civics. He said that if he were on the board, he would propose that a committee meet with all prospective buyers to weed out undesirables."

"Oh, my God! Such bigotry exists here in Arizona?" Barbie exclaimed.

"Yes, it does," Guy responded, "but bigotry can show its ugly head all over. How did you respond to Maxwell on that issue, Don?"

"I told him that the board could not interview anyone with the intent of stopping them from buying into Desert Lakes or any PUD. I asked him if he knew the difference between a PUD and a condominium. And then went on to say that if we were a cooperative and, therefore, shareholders in its corporation we could possibly stop him. I gave, as an example, the famous case where ex-president Nixon was rejected by a cooperative in New York."

"Did that shut him up?" Jamie asked.

"No, then he got even uglier by saying that he guessed then that I had no interest in maintaining property values in Desert Lakes. He said that if I welcomed Blacks, it would only be a short time before Puerto Ricans and queers would be moving in.

"That was too much. What do you mean 'queers,' I practically shouted at him."

"You know, homosexuals, gay people," he said softly as if he were afraid to say it.

"Mister Maxwell," I said, seething. "Do you know that I am homosexual and Robbie Roberts is my lover? We live together. How dare you speak that way?"

"Oh!" Maxwell paused for a moment. "I thought your 'roommate' was a pilot."

"Yes, you idiot, he is a commercial pilot who happens to be homosexual. Now if you'll excuse me, I have to get home to my gay lover." Getting up I took out my wallet and threw a twenty-dollar bill on the table and practically ran out of the restaurant but not before I heard him mumble 'I'm running for the board, you know.'"

"What a son-of-a-bitch!" Barbie shouted.

"So, how did a guy like that get on the board of the HOA?" Guy Neville asked.

"Simple," Cee Jay offered. "Our by-laws say that board members have a three-year term limit, may resign, or in special circumstances may be voted off the board by a majority of its own members. You see, Barbie, in a community such as ours, a lot of people like to complain but few are willing to do the work themselves. I have found that there are three kinds of people who are willing to be on a HOA board: There are those who genuinely want to help their neighbors by doing whatever they can to help. Thank goodness, the majority of board members are good, honest citizens who donate their efforts freely. Some do it just for fun; these people just want to hang out with friends who are also on the board and just want to have something meaningful to do. Unfortunately, there are many, like Maxwell, who join for their own aggrandizement, egos, or gripes. Some in this group are also criminals out to embezzle funds from the HOA treasury or extort money from other residents. This is particularly true in communities such as ours where the HOA handles thousands and potentially, millions of dollars."

"And because of the great variety of condo and homeowner groups," Guy Neville said, "there are no restrictions on who may be on a board. Often, smaller communities find it difficult to even get people to serve on a board. Many board members are appointed before they are elected at an annual meeting. There are no requirements, and most board members serve for as long as they want. After four years, many board members begin to feel as though they own the complex and can do whatever they want."

"Remind me never to live in a community with an HOA," Barbie said.

"Some HOAs are very good for maintaining and operating their communities, but like most organizations in society we, the governed, have to keep watch over those who lead us. If not, all kinds of nut jobs, tyrants, and clowns can take over." Don said. "Let's not forget that our Constitution establishes only three requirements for Representatives: You must be at least twenty-five, be a citizen for seven years, and live in the state you represent." Don paused. "Hey, I qualify!"

All of his guests laughed. "See, I told you that you should run," Cee Jay said.

"And in ten years you can be president," Jamie said. "Imagine. My son Robbie being 'the first husband.' Sounds good, doesn't it, Cee Jay?"

"Sure does, but remember I am Donavon's surrogate father," Cee Jay added.

"I still want to know how Maxwell got on the board," Barbie said.

"Well, we had an opening, and Maxwell volunteered," Cee Jay said. "Don never told the board about his issues with Maxwell, so the board simply appointed him." Cee Jay paused. "But Maxwell didn't last long." "That's right, Barbie. I managed rather quickly and conveniently to get him removed. But in doing so, I gave him a reason to hate me as much as I disliked the weasel." Don said.

"What did you do to get him off the board?" Neville asked.

"Well, during the Easter holidays last year, Joe and Betty Sims were visited by their son and his wife. They arrived from Colorado in their newly purchased RV, which unfortunately would not fit in the Sim's garage which was built for one car and a golf cart. Barb, you and Guy may not know we did build extra- large and high garages for some owners who had RV's as an option. Where possible, some were drive-through, meaning you could enter at one end and exit from the other. They are rather common in the Southwest, particularly with snowbirds.

"So, Sim's son had to park in Joe and Betty's driveway for Holy Week. Well, our Mr. Maxwell did not take kindly to that because our by-laws specifically say that motor vehicles should not remain on the street overnight and not more than one night in a driveway. The founders of our by-laws did not like the way cars parked in the street would make driving down our narrow streets dangerous and disrupt the quaint appearance of our community. They also felt that cars left in the driveway would give our town a 'hunky vibe.' Particularly in the Southwest many broken-up vehicles are left to rust in driveways and can give a neighborhood a bad impression. For the most part, most of our residents were satisfied with this by-law and stayed with it. But Maxwell took matters into his own hands and on Holy Thursday sent the Sims a certified letter stating that the RV parked in their driveway was against the Desert Lakes HOA by-laws and must be immediately removed and, if it was not, Sims would be fined $75.00 for breaking the by-laws and the RV would be reported to the Penal County sheriff's office for removal. The letter looked very impressive

Chuck Walko

because it was typed on our official letterhead stationery. I have a copy of the letter in this file. Maxwell never signed his name or gave anyone else's name. It just said, "The Board would like to know who owns this out-of-state vehicle."

"Hem... Sounds like a very Christian message to send during Easter," Barbie smirked.

"Joe Sims didn't think so. He immediately contacted Randy and started complaining to him. Randy said he knew nothing about the letter and, if he did, would not have approved of it. Randy said that he did not know who wrote it but would immediately look into it. He asked Joe if he could go to his house to make a copy of the letter to share with me and the board members. On behalf of the board, Randy apologized and told Sims to forget about the $75.00 fine.

"Randy then called me. I immediately suspected it might be Maxwell and Randy agreed with me. I suggested that he call for an executive meeting of the entire board, including Maxwell. I told him about A.R.S. title 33, section 1813 which deals with the way a board of directors member may be removed.

"We met on Saturday afternoon and Maxwell did, surprisingly attend. Randy started the meeting by reading the letter. All directors seemed shocked by the letter, but Maxwell readily admitted that he wrote and sent the letter. He said that he felt it was his duty to write it because no one else would. He said that he was fighting for the benefit of Desert Lakes. By-laws he said were being violated 'left and right,' and only he seemed to care to maintain them. I made a note of his specifically saying that he was the only one who seemed to care about what was happening.

May Jones, our secretary, asked him why he wrote that the board wanted to know about this when none of them knew about it. He responded by saying that he was acting on behalf of the board.

"Frank Decker, the vice president, asked him why he didn't bring up the matter with the board first. He said that by the time the board would meet, the vehicle may have been moved and other residents may begin to assume that it was okay to leave any vehicle in a driveway for a long period of time and get away with it. Frank also asked if he had spoken to Sims or anyone at the house before sending the letter. He responded with a flat 'No' and said that he didn't want to get into an argument with Sims.

"Pat O'Brien, our treasurer, then asked him about the $75.00 fine he imposed. Maxwell responded by saying that he thought $75 dollars was significant and just because it would scare Sims to act according to our by-laws. O'Brien then asked him if he just made up the fine to which Maxwell said 'yes.' O'Brien then correctly said, 'Mr. Maxwell, did it occur to you that was an act of extortion, which is actually a crime?'"

Don continued. "Randy then proposed that the board had three alternatives to resolve this very serious matter: First, Mr. Maxwell could personally admit to Sims his mistake and apologize. Second, Mr. Maxwell could be censured or publicly denounced. Third, the board could remove him from office. Then Randy turned to me and asked what my legal opinion was. I told the board that as their attorney I could advise them, but the decision on action was theirs alone to call. I pointed out to them the serious nature of Mr. Maxwell's letter and that it put the board in jeopardy of being sued even though in this case they individually were protected by 'save harmless law.' I then read to them verbatim section 1813 of Statute 33.

"O'Brien then said that the suspicion of extortion was too great for him to abide. He moved to make the motion that Maxwell be removed from office immediately. May Jones seconded the notion; but before it could actually be voted on, Maxwell said that it was too bad that only he seemed to care for the integrity of the board and could save the community; so he would voluntarily immediately resign and save the board from the embarrassment of voting. He then got up and walked out of the room.

"after a pause, Randy said that he would write a formal apology and hand-deliver it to Sims. That case was closed.

"But a few days later, I came to the conclusion that Maxwell was actually a very disturbed man and a possible danger, so I did something that I thought I would never do: I went to a gun shop in Phoenix and purchased a handgun. I certainly never intended to use it, but felt that I might have to. I never told Robbie or anyone else about my fears of some retaliation from Maxwell. I went so far as to take a few lessons on how to use the damn thing."

Don started coughing and indicated that he wanted the glass of water that was on the stand next to his bed. Cee Jay took the glass and held it while Donavon sipped it.

"Are you okay to continue?" Guy Neville asked Don.

"I'm okay. Just a little try from talking too much."

"Listen to him," Barbie smirked. "A lawyer who can't talk." The men chuckled. "Are you able to tell me what the catalyst was that prompted the shooting?" Barbie asked.

After swallowing more water, Don spoke again. "Sure, but Jamie, you may have to help me out if I miss some of the details." He paused briefly to gather his thoughts together and find something in his file on Maxwell.

"One of our residents had solar panels installed on his roof over on Pine Street about a block from Maxwell's house. At the next monthly meeting, of course, Maxwell was there to complain; but this time he had a supporter, Bruce Goldberg. I had seen Bruce around the community. Quite often he was at the golf course or rec center bars or hanging out around the pool. He was a heavyset man who could be heard laughing at his own jokes, which were usually derogatory to women. He always seemed to have an opinion about everything in the news and was prepared to share it with whoever would listen. Robbie jokingly referred to him as 'Mr. Fat-ass Lound-mouth.' Seeing Goldberg with Maxwell, I knew it meant trouble.

"Maxwell stood and turned his back to the board. Instead of addressing the board, he seemed to be appealing to the audience of about fifty residents."

"As I am sure you all know by now," Maxwell began, "the owners of the property at 240 Pine Street have installed solar panels on their roof. Since the board of directors has seemingly no interest in this matter, I am here tonight to tell you why we must demand that these panels must immediately be removed."

Randy immediately cut in. "Mr. Maxwell, if you are here to hold a rally, you are out of order at this meeting. I suggest you hold your own meeting elsewhere." There were a few boos from the audience and Goldberg told Maxwell to go on.

"For the first time in my memory," Don continued, "the board president used his gavel to call for order. Randy instructed him to face the board and address them; if he wished to say anything at this meeting of the board. Maxwell then did turn around to speak.

"Very well, then," Maxwell began. "The board should enforce our bylaws by demanding that the owner of 240 Pine Street remove the solar panels for the following reasons." He held a piece of paper from which he began to read."

Don sifted through his Maxwell file to find a paper. "Here is a copy of what Maxwell read that night. I'll read it to you now, and if you want a copy of it, you may borrow it, Guy."

"First, Solar panels are ugly. They distort the esthetic appearance of the architectural style of the homes in his community.

Second. They lower the value of other homes. We will have a hard time trying to sell our homes because potential buyers don't want to see ugly panels.

Third. The metering box for the panels can be seen by the neighbor whose yard abuts the house and that owner definitely does not appreciate looking at that meter box which is too big and ugly.

Four. Realtors don't even want to show houses with solar panels to prospective buyers because they know that it is a waste of their time. Buyers simply will not even consider a house with panels on the roof.

Five. The owner did not get permission from our HOA Architectural Committee before having the panels installed.

Sixth. It is a well-known fact that solar panels emit radiation which is known to cause cancer, diabetes, ADHD in children.

Seven. Solar panels cause fires which increases insurance rates for everyone.

Eight. Panels can cause the roof to leak. Roof repairs are expensive and once a roof is damaged leaks are inevitable. Roof repairs are very expensive and if the owner can't pay for the necessary repairs, the property will quickly deteriorate, thus bringing down the property values around it.

At the end of this meeting, my colleague, Mr. Bruce Goldberg, and I will be outside handing out a flier containing reasons I just gave for having solar panels banned at Desert Lakes. Thank you. He then sat down as the audience erupted in applause.

Don continued. "I don't know if the applause was for accepting his preposterous claims or for his courage to speak them."

"Randy must have been as dumbfounded as I was. Again, he called for 'order' with his gavel. He thanked Maxwell for his presentation and said that the board would consider what he said and report back at next month's meeting. Randy then asked if Maxwell was aware of Arizona's laws governing the installation of solar panels. Maxwell responded by simply saying, 'I don't have to know any laws. We... and he emphasized the word... simply don't want them here. Again, there was widespread applause. Randy banged the gavel and said the meeting was over." "What planet did that idiot live on? Or when?" Barbie explained.

Donavon started coughing again.

Giving him the glass of water again, Cee Jay asked if he were well enough to finish the story of the shootings. Donavon said that he hoped so and was nearly finished relating all the details to Barbie and Guy.

"The next week Randy called an executive session and asked me if I could attend. Randy asked me to bring my notes and the law books that I had on the use of solar energy in Arizona. I agreed to meet with them.

"The meeting began with some disturbing news. Two of the board members had learned that Goldberg and Maxwell were distributing a petition throughout the community. The petition not only was for their demand that the solar panels should be taken down; but, if they were not, that the board should be replaced by those who would revise the by-laws and make sure solar panels would never be permitted in Desert Lakes. They would also hire a new board lawyer. It was rumored that they had close to 200 signatures already and were aiming for 500 by the time of the next meeting.

"I read aloud to them the statutes that related to solar panels in Arizona and showed that with very few exceptions, the board had absolutely no legal way to enforce Maxwell's absurd demands. They could try, however, to take over the board, but I doubt the Arizona Corporations Commission and the State legislature would allow that on the basis of their illegal demand.

"I warned the board that I would file a civil suit against Maxwell and Goldberg for inciting an insurrection within the community and disturbing the peace. I gave each board member a copy of all pertinent laws. I also suggested that I would be willing to file a suit on behalf of Mr. and Mrs. Jumison, the couple who had installed the solar panels. I told the board that I was confident that the Jumisons would win the case and I would get a lot of publicity for my other political ambitions."

With that pep talk, we began to discuss Maxwell's contentions one by one. His first point was easy to destroy. To say that solar panels are 'ugly' was very subjective. They may have been ugly to him but not to someone else. Research was found that many people at first thought heat pumps, which are combination heating and cooling devices on a roof were ugly at first; but today almost every home in Arizona has one. Years ago, window air conditioners were considered bad because of the noise and their bulk hanging out of a window. Television antennas were also apposed at first and then taken for granted, then replaced by cable and dishes."

His second reason also could quickly be disproven. Solar panels definitely didn't lower the value of a home. We were able to produce evidence from the Board of Realtors that said that solar energy actually increased the value of homes in Arizona by 3 to 4% and that figure was increasing every month as homeowners were saving up to 100% in electric bills. Smart buyers were actually in the market expressly for homes with the panels already installed.

To counter his third proposal, which we all thought was really silly, we suggested that his neighbor plant a bush or a fence that would block their backyard view of the meter box.

Item four was a surprise to us. What realtor would not show a house just because it had solar panels? Assuming that the location, price, and specifications met the buyers' needs, a realtor would be crazy not to show a home just because it had solar. Because homes with solar are already adding five to ten thousand onto a sales price and realtors usually get 6% of that, indeed they would favor showing houses with higher prices.

The fifth objection concerned the fact that the Jumison's did not seek permission from the HOA before they had solar panels installed simply because they didn't have to get anyone's permission. Arizona law clearly implies that a HOA has no control here, even if it wanted to. I told the board that a state cannot take precedence over a federal law and a state law takes precedence over HOA by-laws. I told them that I bet Tesla, which installed the panels, told that to the Jumisons. Speaking of that, I told them that the Federal government was currently subsidizing people for going solar by 26% of the total cost of installation. The U.S., I told them wants to eliminate fossil energy by 2035.

"California is succeeding other states because of the forward-thinking policies of the state legislature. California is currently circulating a bill that would mandate solar systems in all new homes built after 2020. The bill will become law in 2018 and is effective in 2020. California will start enforcing Title 24 in 2023. The California Clean Energy Commission predicts that it may cost a single homeowner about $8,400 and will pay for itself in savings on electric bills in five to ten years. I showed the board a chart which showed that in this past year of 2012 the solar market in the U.S. increased by 76%. As long ago as 1999 the City of Scottsdale covered 8500 square feet of a parking lot with panels to provide parking shade as well as produce 93 kilowatts of energy.

"Someone should ask Maxwell, who comes from the state of Washington, if he knows that Arizona has more days of sunshine than any other state.

"Randy asked what Maxwell was referring to when he claimed that our HOA had an 'Architectural Committee' that should have been consulted. I explained that there never was one, but Maxwell may have been referring to the CC & R's which do state that future structures built by firms other than Roberts Development must be approved by an architectural committee appointed by the Roberts company. My father-in-law and I wanted Desert Lakes to adhere to that Southwestern style of architecture. Furthermore, solar panels certainly don't affect the architectural style of any home."

"May Jones wanted to know if there was evidence that linked solar panels to cancer, diabetes, and attention deficit disorders. None of us had ever heard of any scientific study about it. I told the group that I had heard of a study in New Jersey that showed there was a connection between cancer and people living in homes near big, high wire poles. Randy said that he heard something about that also in Lake Havasu. Such studies relating to solar must have been undertaken for the federal and state governments to endorse solar so vigorously.

Maxwell probably created this myth himself or got it from some conspiracy theorist who was against solar energy. There are a lot of crackpot conspiracy people who enjoy that sort of thing.

Just to play it safe, however, I advised May to look into it more.

"We dismissed Maxwell's seventh and eighth items rather quickly. We put the burden of proof that solar panels cause fires on him. He would have to show us the statistics that indicate this preposterous claim. All installers of solar panels guarantee their work against leaks. The standard is a minimum of seven years. All roofs, with or without solar, must be maintained. No roof will last forever, particularly in the blistering Arizona sun. Panels can actually protect a roof from deteriorating.

"We felt confident that we could counter all of Maxwell and Goldberg's arguments and were ready for the meeting. Our concerns shifted to the community. Could we convince the homeowners that solar panels were acceptable and that Maxwell's arguments were fallacious?

We knew that solar energy was a relatively new concept and those over fifty-five were skeptical and cautious. We feared that there might be trouble, certainly emotions would flare and there might be shouting and yelling.

Pat O'Brien suggested that we call for help from the Sheriff's office, but Randy felt that having a uniformed officer with a gun showing in his holster would only add to the tensions and doubts that people would have. We live in a peaceful community, he said. Let's try to keep it that way intelligently. I did not express any fear to the board, but inwardly I was a wreck. I stepped up my sessions at the rifle range and hope that Robbie would not attend the meeting. When I learned that he was given the job of flying the charter to Jamaica, I was overjoyed."

Don turned to Cee Jay. He smiled. "Dad, remember I called you that afternoon to tell you about that movie on Turner Classics and suggested that you stay home and watch it rather than going to the HOA meeting? I deliberately didn't want you there."

"Jamie, I'm tired, and I'm finding it difficult to talk more. I think it would be better if you gave Barbie, Cee Jay, and Guy your impressions as a witness to the event rather than me." "Sure thing, partner," Jamie said.

"But before you begin, let me say that I also called Mom and tried to convince her to watch **The Sun Also Rises** with Cee Jay, but she refused. She wanted to be at your side at the meeting. She said she would be my silent cheerleader. "Donavon's eyes started tearing and he asked for more water.

"Well, Don has done a great job of telling you what led up to the meeting," Jamie began.

"I don't have much more to tell you except the crowd was much bigger than I expected and that kind of scared me. The silence and tensions were palpable in the room. Normally, as Don told you before, we would have 30 or so people at a HOA meeting. That night there must have been at least 100; it really was standing room only. Melissa and I sat near the back and tried to be as innocuous as possible. A few people that knew us smiled and others politely asked how we were, but I knew that deep down they were confused about why the developer was there.

Maxwell and Greenberg were together in the front row center. I noticed that Maxwell seemed nervous. He was very pale and looked sick. He was like a man who hadn't slept in a while. Mr. Fat-ass was dressed well; this was the first time I ever saw him in a suit. He was, as usual, loud and laughing with a few friends. On his lap was a pile of papers that I assumed were the petitions.

Donavon was at a small table on the far left separated from the head table. The five members of the Board were present with Randy in the center. Approximately ten feet separated the president from Maxwell and his sidekick, Mr. Fat-ass Loud-mouth, as Robbie called him.

"At exactly 8:00 Randy hit the gavel and announced that the HOA Board of Desert Lakes, Arizona, was now in session. He started the meeting, as usual, by asking the secretary to read the minutes of the previous meeting. After they were read and approved, he welcomed all the people who were attending perhaps for the first time. He then introduced each member and said a little bit about each one.

"Randy then said that there would be no new business at this meeting because they only had one important issue on the agenda for that meeting, He did say that the board had an executive meeting and were prepared to respond to Mr. Maxwell's request concerning the solar panels on the house at 240 Pine Street. "Before we do that, however," Randy said, "we understand that a petition has been circulated in the community. Mr. Maxwell, would you like to present that petition to us at this time?

"Mr. Maxwell is not feeling well tonight, Randy, so I will be representing him today. Yes, we have 262 signed petitions here. All of them are signed by residence who support our position against solar panels." He returned to his seat after dumping them on the table in front of Randy. I took notice of the fact that he referred to the board president as 'Randy' rather than Mr. Scott, as was customary at our board meetings. I interpreted this as a sign that Fat-ass was trying to show his superiority over Randy at that point.

"Randy maintained his composure. He thumbed through several of the petitions and then handing the pile down to May said,' Madame Secretary, please note in the minutes that Mr. Goldberg delivered 262 petitions by residents. Mr. Maxwell or Mr. Greenberg, would either of you wish to say anything more.'

"No," Goldberg said, "We believe that the petitions speak for us and the majority of Desert Lakes residents. So, it's your turn to tell us what you are going to do. Go ahead, Randy, tell us what you got to say."

"I got to tell you, kids," Jamie said, "at that point, I felt like getting up and punching that smart ass son-of-a-bitch right in the keister. Who the hell did he think he was? His whole demeanor disgusted me. He acted like a New York mafia boss, which he may have been"

Randy continued nice and calm, but forceful. "Ladies and gentlemen, I understand how you may feel about this matter. I appreciate the effort that Mr. Maxwell and Mr. Goldberg have exhibited in making their feelings heard and I admire the civic pride that you have shown through this petition and your attendance at tonight's meeting. I am happy that so many of you are here. Keep on coming to all our meetings.

That's how we do things in a civilized society.

"I have prepared a newsletter which will be printed tomorrow and mailed to all residents at the expense of our HOA treasury. In this newsletter, I, on behalf, of the entire board must reject your request to change our by-laws and demand that the owners at 240 Pine Street remove their solar panels. I want all of you here tonight and all residents of Desert Lakes to know that if we did so, we would be derelict in our duty to preserve our values as a community and we all could be considered criminals. That's right: criminals because we would be in violation of Arizona State Law which homeowners who decide to go solar. Indeed, I can tell you that in a few years this entire conversation on this issue will be antiquated, and many of us will, in the not too distant future, be purchasing solar energy ourselves. I don't think any of us would want to give up our air conditioning, would we? Well, not too, too long ago, folks were talking about central air conditioners on their roofs the way many of us today feel about solar panels now. Clean energy is coming, folks, and it's coming fast here in Arizona, the sunniest state in the Union, So we should welcome it, not protest against it. I'm sure you all want lower electric bills and to live in a world where clean energy means we can all live better without pollution."

Randy continued. "The Board's newsletter will explain why many of Mr. Maxwell's concerns are just plain wrong. Consider seriously what we say in the newsletter, and if you still feel that you want a new membership on the board and new by-laws, I welcome you to do so. Your present board will gladly give up their free services to you. And Don. Rice, who has been working diligently without any compensation as our attorney, will be also happy to turn things over to someone you may hire and pay through potential raises in the rec center fees. Please go home now peacefully and calmly and thank God that you live in this beautiful community." He banged the gavel and said, "This meeting is now over."

It was at that moment that Maxwell jumped up. He seemed to wabble as he circled in front of the table. "Oh, no, Mr. Big shot president, we're not going to let you get away without respecting our wishes. You're going to have to pay for that!" he shouted, pulling a gun from his pocket. The audience gasped as he pointed the gun at Randy. "I'll teach you!" Then he shot Randy in the face at close range. I'm sure that Randy died instantly.

Then he pointed the gun at Don. His last words were: "And you, you destroyed this Board, you faggot!" he shouted and pulled the trigger at seemingly the same instant Don pulled his. Maxwell seemed to hesitate for a moment and then his body collapsed on the floor. Don fell over the small table and then onto the floor.

As you may expect, everyone was in a state of shock. People were yelling and screaming.

There was blood all over the floor and parts of Randy's face were blown across the wall. I saw two men that I thought were doctors go to the bodies and told everyone to stay away. I grabbed Melissa who was screaming, but I couldn't move her, so I ran out of the room to an office to call 911. As I was entering the office, I noticed Goldberg running out of the building.

"After I made the call to 911, I went back into the room to get Melissa who still seemed to be in shock. Most people had left the room and were slowly milling around outside or got into their cars to get away quickly from the horror they experienced. It was like a nightmare. I went up to the two guys who were protecting the bodies. We just stared at one another for a long time. We couldn't speak. At last, I turned to Don's body which was in a pool of blood. I remember asking the man if he were a doctor. He nodded that he was. Then I told him that Don was my son-in-law. I asked if he thought he was still alive. The guy told me that there still was a weak pulse.

I got the help of a man who also was still in the room. Together we pulled and practically carried Melissa out of the room.

The ambulances and police cars arrived in minutes. Medics began working on the three victims. I was later told by the police that Randy and Maxwell were declared dead. There was a possibility that Don would make it. Melissa and I waited until Don was in the ambulance, then we picked up Cee Jay and rushed to the hospital to keep vigil.

"You gave all of quite a scare, young man," Jamie said rubbing Don's head.

Jamie turned to the reporter. "Guy, you were at the hospital that night also, weren't you?"

"Yes, I was with another reporter from the Casa Grande newspaper. I was with *the Star* from Tucson."

"We should be going now," Cee Jay said. "Let's let our hero here have some rest."

At that moment a nurse entered the room. "Mr. Roberts and Mr. Neville?"

Together both said "Yes"...

"There is a man out in the hall who says that it is very important that he speak to both of you immediately. He seems quite adamant to see both of you now.

"Who is he? Guy asked.

"He said his name was Bill Gonzales."

Guy turned to Jamie. "That's the reporter from the Casa Grande paper. Let's see what he wants."

Bill Gonzales was waiting for them at the nurses' station down the hall. "I'm sorry to disturb your visit with Mr. Rice, but our afternoon edition just came out, and I rushed over here to give this to you. He held up the paper to his chest.

The headline in big lettering on the front page was:

**Coroner Says "Rice Didn't Kill
Desert Lakes HOA Madman"**

"What the hell!" Guy exclaimed.

Bill gave each man a paper and held on to one for himself. Both Jamie and Guy quickly scanned the story which bore Gonzales's by line.

Jamie's eye caught keywords and phrases: *Coroner... autopsy... massive heart attack... Rice just inflicted a minor wound... could not have killed... HOA madman... wife says... Maxwell treated for heart disease... high blood pressure... Opioids found in blood...*

"Holy shit!" Jamie exclaimed. "This news is amazing!"

Jamie hugged the reporter. "Come on... let's break the story to Don."

As the three men entered the room, Jamie joyfully shouted, "Don, meet Bill Gonzales, your new best friends."

Bill went to Don's bedside and shook his left hand.

Don smiled and said, "Ah, Hi, Bill. So why are you my new best friend?"

Gonzales gave him his newspaper as Jamie gave his to his daughter, and Guy gave his paper to Cee Jay. There was a minute of silence as everyone read the story and began to contemplate its implications. They looked at one another and then Don who was blinking his eyes and shaking his head.

Barbie was the first to speak. "So... what does this mean?"

"Well, for starters," Jamie said, "it means that Don needs more practice at the rifle range."

"It means we should start calling Don Congressman Rice," Guy Neville said.

"It means we should go home and spread the news to Robbie and Melissa and let our hero here get some rest," Cee Jay said. "Everybody out!"

Slowly, everyone said goodbye and filed out of the room. Guy Neville was the last to leave. He kissed Don's forehead while holding his good hand firmly. "I hope you do become a Representative, Don. The country needs you."

Don smiled. "Well, if I do, you are going to be my campaign manager and press secretary, Guy." He paused. "Or my editor when this 'country lawyer' writes his first book."

"That's not a bad idea. You would be a good writer. What will your book be about?"

Don closed his eyes and softly said, "murder at Desert Lakes HOA."

About the Author

Chuck has been a teacher, administrator, real estate appraiser and broker. He served as an education association leader and has been on the board of three HOA's. Chuck also worked as the property manager for a fourth, landmark condo association in Tucson.

He has taught students in grades seven through twelve in suburban and inner-city schools as well as private preparatory schools. He also has been an adjunct professor at several colleges in New Jersey and Arizona.

A native of New Jersey, he has also lived in Long Island, New York, and Arizona. He is now retired and calls New Mexico, his "land of enchantment." Chuck's passions are life-long learning, reading, movies and theater, writing, and physical fitness.

Other books by Chuck Walko

Greenwich Village Tales

Most of these "tales" take place during the 1960s and shed light on the gay scene in New York during that period of change. Cee Jay Seton is the narrator of these fictitious accounts of a diversity of men he meets in a neighborhood hangout bar in Greenwich Village, New York. Perhaps the most prominent character in the book is Jamie Roberts, a hustler who eventually becomes Cee Jay's life-long partner.

These stories are serious, humorous, touching, and even tragic.

Robbie Keeps the Key

Robbie Roberts, a star basketball player, is shocked to learn that his father, Jamie, is bisexual; and that dad's lover is a popular teacher, Dr. Cee Jay Seton. Robbie's confusion increases when he meets and befriends the quarterback Donavon Rice, who has a reputation for being a great kisser. Don eventually takes Robbie's sister, Barbie, to their senior prom. This novel explores cultural standards in a fast-moving and tender story, with some comedy and a bit of explicit gay sex.

Printed in the United States
by Baker & Taylor Publisher Services

Printed in the United States
by Baker & Taylor Publisher Services